Loathing a Landon

The Barrington Billionaires

Book Twelve

Ruth Cardello

Author Contact

website: RuthCardello.com
email: ruthcardello@gmail.com
Facebook: Author Ruth Cardello
Twitter: RuthieCardello
Goodreads
goodreads.com/author/show/4820876.Ruth_Cardello
Bookbub
bookbub.com/authors/ruth-cardello

Dedication

This book is dedicated to my friend Carol.
Everyone needs a friend they can call who'll meet them
at midnight
with a shovel and zero questions.

Note to the readers: I created Festner's disease in my imagination based on research I did on hereditary diseases that could be treated in utero. It is, however, a completely fictitious disease. As someone who lost a niece to SIDs, I know the devastation it leaves in its wake. My heart goes out to any family who has experienced it. I've heard researchers are closing in on a cause and I pray they are able to protect all babies in the future from it.

Copyright

Chapter One

Amanda Glenford

Present Day

I DON'T KNOW anyone who likes sitting in a cloth gown in a doctor's office waiting for test results and I am no different. After two weeks of not feeling well, though, I'd done an online search of what my symptoms might be indicative of and let's just say that had been a mistake.

Paranasal tumors?

Leukemia?

Hemophilia?

I'd had a nosebleed or two as a child, but never like the ones I'd had over the past two weeks. Add a nearly constant headache, a sudden loss of appetite, bouts of lightheadedness and I'd gladly agreed to a full examination with extensive blood work.

Stress could do funny things to a person, and I'd definitely had more than my fair share of that lately. After college, I'd moved away from my hometown to start my own website design and marketing company in the city. I went home several times a year and for all the holidays, but life had gotten busy and my visits less frequent. Speaking to my parents on the phone weekly had felt like enough.

However, a few weeks ago, I'd given in to an impulse, canceled some meetings and headed home with the intention of surprising my parents. Imagine my shock when what I found was my mother resting after a chemotherapy treatment.

Chemotherapy.

For a battle with breast cancer no one had told me about.

My entire world crashed in with the news. How had I missed something that big? Why didn't she feel she could rely on me to be there for her? What kind of daughter was I if she thought I would rather not know?

She said she was over the worst of it. The doctors were optimistic. In her usual style, she assured me she was fine, but my heart broke a hundred times as I realized how many opportunities I'd missed to show her how much I loved her.

Nothing I'd built in the city mattered more to me than my family. I decided right then and there that I'd move back home and bring as much of my business with me as I could. I didn't tell my parents my plans because they would have told me it wasn't necessary.

They loved me unselfishly, but that didn't mean they didn't deserve better than I'd given them. Maturity and time away had changed my perspective on many things. They'd always encouraged me to follow my dreams even when those dreams had taken me away from them. That was the way I wanted to love . . .

When I asked my father how the hardware store was doing, he said, "Good. Cooper has kept everything going."

Cooper.

The mere mention of his name sent a flood of mixed emotions through me. He'd been part of our lives ever since my father had come home with reddened knuckles and told us about a young man he'd caught breaking into our family's store.

Cooper had been a scrawny, troubled teenager, so broken that my father had gone against my mother's advice and given him a job as well as the one-room apartment above the hardware store. I'd been angry with Cooper for attacking my father until I'd met him. Gaunt, covered in old bruises, in torn clothing that was brown in parts from dried blood— he'd looked like someone who'd escaped something horrific.

I helped my mother cook meals for Cooper even though I'd never been good in the kitchen and helped my father choose clothing for Cooper. Before our eyes Cooper transformed from scared and angry to my father's helpful shadow. My father taught him how to do everything from stock his store to frame buildings. Cooper wanted to learn it all and wasn't above any chore. Have an issue with something mechanical or taking down a rotting tree? Cooper would handle it for you. It was impossible to go home and not hear about something he'd done for someone.

Collectively the people in Driverton went along with the story that Cooper was the son of one of my father's old Army buddies even though they all knew it was a lie. The truth was no one knew where Cooper had come from or what had happened to him there.

When I'd moved away, it was harder to forget about Cooper than I'd imagined it would be. He'd always been there, a silent protector, making sure I made it home from parties or dates. I joked that he was the reason I was still a virgin when I'd headed off to college.

All the manual labor had quickly given Cooper a body women drooled over and men respected. Even in high school it had been difficult to find anyone willing to date me with him looking on. He was strong, quiet, and a little dangerous.

He could have dated any of the single women in our town, but he didn't. My high school friends said it was because of me. I'd stopped believing that a long time ago.

Despite how long I'd been away and the fact that I'd had relationships since, I still thought about him too often, still missed how safe his presence had made me feel.

Ridiculous?

Maybe, but that didn't change how frequently I wondered if he missed me as well.

Turning to him for comfort the night I'd learned about my mother's cancer had been a bad decision. Having sex with him had been as well. I'd woken alone and learned from my father that he'd left town—like I meant nothing to him, because I obviously didn't.

The door of the examination room opened and my doctor entered with a laptop. She was polished, efficient, and completely unreadable as far as my diagnosis. "Sorry about the wait, Amanda. I needed to double-check something on your records."

"That's fine." I folded my hands on my lap. "What did

you need to double-check?"

She placed the laptop on a small table beside the examination table. "You had genetic testing done as an infant."

"Yes. On my father's side there were several cases of sudden infant death. The cause was determined to be Festner's disease. There was no treatment for it and the mortality rate was a hundred percent if both parents had the gene." I swallowed hard. Was it possible that the gene had morphed into one that caused issues later on? "Is my condition related to that? My mother didn't have the gene so I was told the trait is recessive in me."

My doctor nodded. "It is." She looked down at her laptop then met my gaze. "When was your last menstrual cycle?"

Oh, my God, it's affecting my cycle as well? "Two weeks ago?" It had been different—lighter than usual.

"And the last sexual intercourse you engaged in?"

My cheeks warmed and I looked away. I was actively doing my best to forget about that mistake. "Three weeks ago?"

Fingers poised above her laptop keyboard, she asked, "You're not sure?"

I was, I just didn't want it to be true. I rubbed a hand across my eyes. "Three weeks. I don't see what this has to do with why I'm here."

"Amanda, you're pregnant."

"No." I wasn't accepting that. "I'm not."

"I'm afraid you are."

"I can't be," I protested. Not now. Not with Cooper. When my doctor didn't say anything, I added, "I'm on the pill."

"Nothing outside of abstinence is one hundred percent effective."

I knew that, but I wasn't supposed to be in the percentile it didn't work for. I buried my face in my hands as memories from the night I'd been trying so hard to forget began flooding back. Cooper's mouth on mine, hot and demanding. Our bodies intimately entangled. Of course it had come with a cost.

No. I refused to be having a baby with a man who didn't care enough to be there when I woke up in the morning, a man who'd been avoiding me ever since. I'd been home to see my parents and each time he'd been "still out of town on business." Cooper's only job was at my family's hardware store. He didn't have business out of town. I lowered my hands. Worse, people knew we'd been together. Not that Cooper or I had said anything. Someone must have seen my car parked at the hardware store overnight. That's all it took in my hometown for people to decide we were a couple. We weren't.

What's the opposite of together? That's what Cooper and I were.

"Are you sure?"

"Yes." There was sympathy in the doctor's eyes.

"Oh, my God. I can't do this." *Not with everything else going on.* I hadn't realized I'd spoken some of it aloud until she answered me.

"There are options . . ."

"No." I didn't want a baby, but I wanted that even less.

"I'll figure it out."

After a pause, she added, "I realize this has been a shock, but we do need to talk about the fact that you carry a recessive gene for Festner's. There are treatments now that if started early enough have proven highly effective. I'll give you the number of the OB/GYN here. Together we'll come up with a plan for how to move forward. Ideally, you'd start gene therapy in utero . . . during the first trimester. So, the clock is ticking. There are tests she can run on the fetus, but not any without possible side effects. The best course of action is to quickly confirm if the biological father also carries the recessive gene."

"Confirm?"

"It's a simple blood draw. Our lab can rush the results in cases like this. If you could have him come in to the office tomorrow, I could have an answer for you within days."

"Tomorrow?" I asked in a strangled voice. I wasn't ready for any part of this. "I don't know if that'll be possible." Cooper didn't own a cell phone. Crazy, right? He'd made Driverton his world. For as long as I could remember, he'd never had a television, computer, or phone. He said he preferred to read, and his shelves as well as all corners of his apartment were filled with books on every topic from ancient to modern. The number of how-to books that man owned would put most libraries to shame. The same could be said for his collection of classics.

Sympathy filled my doctor's eyes again. "I take it you're not with the father."

I blinked back tears and took a deep breath. "I'm not."

"Do you have a way to contact him?"

I let out a shaky breath. "I think so." My father had suggested this wasn't the first time Cooper had disappeared. Someone back home had to know where he was.

"Normally I wouldn't discuss when or if you should inform the biological father, but if you feel that you can't involve him, you should schedule testing for the fetus this week. The sooner you know if gene therapy is needed the better."

Swallowing hard, I nodded and placed a hand on my still flat stomach. *I'm having a baby. Me. A mother.* I thought about my own and what she would have done in this situation. "He'll be here." *I'll make it happen.*

"I'll give you paperwork. He won't need to schedule a time—just show up."

"He will."

She wrote out a paper and handed it to me. "I added the information for the OB/GYN."

"Thank you." I accepted it and stuffed it in my purse then pointed to my face. "What about my nosebleeds?"

"Perfectly normal for some pregnant women."

"And the loss of appetite? The dizziness?"

"All normal. Your OB/GYN will have the latest suggestions on how to alleviate those symptoms, but I'll email you some things that worked for me. Moving forward, I'll stay in the loop as much or as little as you want me to." She placed a hand on my arm. "If you want to talk to someone I can write a referral for that as well. You're going to be okay."

I sniffed and made an attempt at a joke. "I came in

thinking I had leukemia, so I guess this is good news."

She smiled kindly. "I have four children and there have been hard days, but never any so bad that I regretted having them."

"Four?" My hand returned to my stomach. I couldn't imagine. The idea of one was overwhelming.

My head was still spinning as I made my way out of the office to my car. Once inside I sat there holding the steering wheel without starting the engine.

Looks like I'm going home.

Again.

Chapter Two

Cooper

Three weeks earlier

I'D GO UP there with you, but you know I hate heights," Ollie Williams called from the bottom of a ladder he'd held as I'd climbed it to access the roof of Little Willie's, the only pub within twenty miles of the small town we both lived in.

Driverton, Maine, was lucky to be mentioned on a map. An old logging town that had lost most of its inhabitants after the sawmill closed, it boasted a population of less than two hundred people. With nothing to lure tourists and no large employers, it remained a mostly closed community. Many of its young people left for college, often swearing they'd never return, only to do so when they started their own families.

It was a town outside of time. A small number of newcomers stumbled upon the town and stayed—like me. People didn't lock their doors and children ran free because people watched out for each other. Several decades ago the population had been homogeneous, but that had shifted over time to a more eclectic mix of cultures and races. According to the news it shouldn't work as well as it did, but I wouldn't try telling anyone in Driverton that their differences were a problem.

Winters had them hunkering in and relying on each other in a way that bred trust. Policing was covered by a neighboring sheriff's office, but not enough happened in the area for them to waste resources coming by unless summoned.

The last time anyone had called the police? Five years back a rowdy group of college kids had rolled into town. They'd gone into Little Willie's and made some crude comments to Ollie's young cousin Katie who was waiting tables that day. It didn't take more than that to get everyone in the pub on their feet.

Fists started flying. Glass started breaking. I wasn't there that day, but heard it was one of the college kids who called 911. Someone should have warned him that Katie was the sheriff's little sister. It didn't turn out well for them.

Driverton had a reputation for not being welcoming, but that was far from the truth. They'd taken me in when I'd had nowhere to go and not a cent to my name.

"Stay where you are," I said as I made my way across the roof to where a couple of shingles had flown off during the last storm. After assessing the damage, I added, "It's an easy fix this time, but you need to replace the whole roof before winter." We'd had a similar conversation a few months earlier, so I wasn't overly hopeful he'd take action this time either.

"A new roof isn't in the budget this year."

It needed to be. "I'll buy the shingles. If we do it on a Saturday, Everette and Levi can help me." There weren't too many young men left in the town so when something needed to be done we all pitched in.

"Don't do that. I'll talk to the bank."

I replaced the shingles without responding then headed back down the ladder. We both knew what the bank's response would be. Ollie's father had been one of the nicest men I'd ever come across, but that hadn't made him good with finances. When he died a year back he'd left not only the bar, but a crippling amount of debt and a wife who had no idea she was broke.

No one had the heart to tell her. Mrs. Williams was the first to bring soup to the sick and was the last to leave a party because she was compelled to help clean up afterward. She could soothe any screaming baby, treated minor injuries as well as the urgent care that was nearly an hour's drive, and stop a grown man mid-swear with a stern look.

I don't have many memories of my own mother, but I often wondered if they would have had anything in common. I doubted it. In the world I'd been born to, nannies raised the babies, doctors came to a person's house, and morality was an outdated idea.

"I don't want your money, Cooper," Ollie stressed.

I took the ladder from him and returned it to the back of my truck. "We'll be here early Saturday. Hopefully you'll be able to open for dinner."

"I'll find a way to pay you back—every dollar."

When I'd first come to town, Ollie's parents had decided I was too thin and had made it their mission to fatten me up. They'd told me lunch at Little Willie's would always be free for me. Over the years I'd likely eaten more than the cost of the shingles. "You've prepaid me with sandwiches." He still looked about to argue, so I added, "One or two of your mother's berry pies and we'll be even."

"Okay, but . . ." Ollie shook his head. "If you continue to be so generous with your money you'll never move out from above the hardware store."

"Why would I want to? It's convenient and I don't need more than a bed."

He gave me a long look that had me looking away. "Thank you. You're a good friend. If you ever need anything . . ."

I nodded once. Like his father, Ollie would give me his last dollar . . . if he had one. He called me his brother from another mother. I wondered what he'd call me if I told him that everything he thought he knew about me was a lie. I wasn't Cooper Davis. I wasn't twenty-eight. My social security number and birth certificate were forgeries.

Survival had necessitated letting go of the past as well as any thought of a future. I lived in the moment, focused on being the best person I could be, and found manual labor quieted the noise in my head.

I'd become so good at lying that there were times I almost believed I really was the son of an old Army buddy of Pete Glenford who had come to visit the Glenfords and decided to stay because I liked the town. Almost.

Nothing good came from wishing any part of my journey had been different. People threw the word redemption around like it was possible for everyone who sought it, but it wasn't.

I'd seen the darkest corners of my soul and there was no way back from that.

No matter how much I might want there to be.

An image of Pete's daughter Amanda flashed in my head as if to prove that point. I cursed then swore again when I pinched one of my fingers beneath a strap while securing the ladder. Amanda was where she should be, living the life she deserved, and likely happily dating any number of men who were a whole lot better for her than I ever could be.

Pete and his family had been far too good to me for me to ever allow myself more than the passing fantasy of being with his daughter. She was everything I was not—adventurous, optimistic . . . so damn full of potential and spirit.

And beautiful.

Painfully so.

She'd always accused me of not liking her; that couldn't have been further from the truth. I hated the idea of her with anyone else, but hated the idea of her with me even more.

Know thyself.

I did and I had nothing I could offer anyone beyond my anger. There were many days when I woke slightly disappointed that I'd been gifted another day.

Not every day though. No, I came alive every few months when Sheriff Tom came to see me because a teenager had gone missing somewhere in New England. He recommended my services to families when others began to tell them that nothing more could be done. I was skilled at tracking runaways because I knew what it was like to be on the run.

I could talk a teen into going home if that was a safe option for them. I could free them from most situations because I wasn't held back by legalities. Tom didn't ask how I brought the kids home and that was for the best. I left no fingerprints, no digital footprint . . . nothing that could be traced back to me.

The families who could afford it sent money to me through Tom. We put those funds toward helping the next child. Using cash instead of credit cards kept me invisible and that was how I intended to remain.

My unconventional partnership with Tom had started when Katie's out-of-town boyfriend had convinced her to run away with him. Although she'd agreed at first, he'd turned violent once he had her out of town and alone. She'd managed to leave a frightened message on her brother's phone and the news had spread like wildfire through our town.

Something in me had snapped when Tom had asked the locals if we'd help look for her. *Look? No, find.* There was no other outcome I could accept. I found her first. When I saw the bruises on Katie's face I let loose my fury on her boyfriend, a man who was two years older than I was and several inches taller. Pete's arrival on the scene was the only reason that man lived. Pete held me back, calmed the monster within me, and then we both stopped Tom from finishing what I'd started when he arrived.

None of us spoke of that day, but I'd made an impression on the sheriff side of Tom because he and I had covertly worked together ever since without killing a single soul.

See, I have goals. Ten years, no kills. And a purpose . . .

"You okay?" Ollie asked.

I wasn't, but I couldn't remember a time when I had been. "Just trying to remember what Pete asked me to pick up on my way back."

That wasn't entirely a lie. Pete had driven into the city with his wife, Dotty, for what the doctors said might be her last cycle of chemotherapy treatment. As long as the test came back with the news we were all waiting to hear, the worst of Dotty's battle was behind her.

Each treatment had worn her out more than the last, so we'd been told to expect her to be exhausted for a week or so this time. As I'd done after each of Dotty's treatments, I'd made sure there was a hearty meal for Pete when they returned as well as ginger ale, saltines, and a light soup for Dotty. Pete tended to not eat well leading up to her treatments. It was only when she was home again, tucked in and resting, that his appetite returned.

Ollie smiled. "Tell Dotty my mom will drop over tomorrow to check in on her."

"Will do." I made my way to the driver's side of my truck.

"Hey, Cooper."

I'd opened my door and paused to turn back to face him.

"Yes?"

"Thanks for today. I know you're already doing extra at the store. With the rain coming tonight . . ."

I finished climbing into my truck, shut the door, then drove off without so much as a wave. I was good to Ollie because he and his family had always been good to me. If he needed more from me than that, he'd forever be disappointed.

And he wouldn't be the only one.

A memory from years earlier came back to me. It was from the night I'd taken Amanda to her senior prom. We'd danced too close long enough for me to forget all the reasons I was wrong for her.

On the drive home, one kiss had led to another until I'd parked and our clothing had started flying off. When she'd whispered, "I always knew you liked me," I'd frozen and regained enough control to stop.

In desperation, I'd thrown her shirt back at her and said, "You're wrong." I didn't like her, I loved her, at least as much as someone like me could love anyone. In a poor attempt to explain why I needed to take her home rather than continue what we'd started, I said, "I only took you to the prom because your father asked me to."

She'd started crying then. Guilt and shame had overtaken my ability to comfort her. As a parting remark when she'd exited my car in front of her house, she'd snarled, "Do me a favor and walk the other way when you see me. I can't wait to get out of this town and away from you."

I'd done my best to respect that request ever since. Over

the years, when she came home to visit her parents, I made sure I was somewhere else.

She saw that as a snub.

It wasn't.

Amanda belonged with someone who was as wholesome and loving as she was. I wanted her to find a man who'd make her happy. I also wanted to never have to meet him.

Chapter Three

Amanda

THE DRIVE TO Maine was just long enough to remind me why weekly video chats had so often replaced visiting my parents in person. Coming home was always confusing.

I told myself I loved living in the city. I could date who I wanted, work whatever hours my job required without judgement, change my circle of friends when a change was needed—all without having to hear what anyone thought about my decisions.

Growing up in a tight-knit community might sound wonderful, but it had its negatives as well. There's a reason people say you can't be a prophet in your own town. In Driverton, it was difficult to be more than Pete and Dotty's daughter—a nice, reliable girl who would eventually move home and take over her father's store. Even years after I'd moved away, despite the fact that I'd done well for myself in the city, every trip home included someone asking me: "So are you thinking about moving back? Settling down?" or worse: "Have you seen Cooper? He's still single."

It was the mention of Cooper that sent my mood sideways a bit and my response was always the same: "I'm not moving back. I have no desire to start a family. I haven't seen Cooper in years, but I'm sure he's as happy with his life as I am with mine." That didn't stop people from mentioning him to me. From my sixth-grade teacher, Miss Kean, to the postmaster . . . they were relentless.

It didn't help that I wasn't as happy in the city as I'd once been. Business-wise, the move had made sense. I'd made the contacts necessary to get my business off the ground. I was fit and trim from my strict gym schedule. My social schedule was full of dates with men I wasn't particularly attached to and people who would best be described as "situational friends."

People invited me to parties, wine tastings, even group vacations. We had fun together, but that was as deep as it went. I didn't have someone I felt comfortable enough to call to pick up something from the pharmacy or to sit quietly beside me when I was sad.

Recently I'd won five thousand dollars on a scratch ticket and had no one beyond my parents to call with that news, no one I knew would genuinely be happy for me.

That realization had left me feeling a little off-kilter. How could I have so many people in my life and still feel lonely?

I thought about the people who had meant the most to me and they were all back in Driverton. There were so many times I almost called one of them, but so much time had gone by I was afraid it would be awkward. "Hey, sorry I didn't return your text . . . I meant to. It's only been what . . . one . . . *three* years? That long? Yeah. That's a long time to forget to answer you."

It was no wonder that they'd stopped coming around to see me when I went to visit my parents. Even Cooper made himself scarce when I was around. It wasn't a great feeling and probably part of the reason so much time had gone by since I'd been home.

Six months.

Way too long.

That must be why I'd woken with the gut feeling that I needed to drive home. The feeling had been strong enough I'd cleared my schedule for the day, filled my gas tank and hit the interstate.

The closer I got to my parents' house, the more emotional I became. Mrs. Williams smiled and waved from her front porch. I saw one of my old best friends pushing a stroller into the park as I drove past. Mel and Mike had married right out of high school and according to my parents were on their third child. I knew their children's names only because my parents kept me up to date on their lives. It was strange to feel like an outsider in my own hometown.

There was an old truck in my parents' driveway. I recognized it as the one my father had owned before he'd given it to Cooper. Heart racing, hands suddenly cold, I hated how much of an effect Cooper still had on me.

Eight years. I should have been over him.

He should be over avoiding me.

Okay, yes, I'd told him I never wanted to see him again, but I'd been hurt, angry, and *in high school.* All he'd achieved by respecting that demand was to ensure that we never got past the night I'd thrown myself at him and he'd—ducked.

We're both adults now. I'm going to walk in there, shake his hand, and tell him it's good to see him. This doesn't have to be awkward.

I parked behind his truck, cut the engine, took a deep breath, then stepped out of my car. To my surprise my parents didn't immediately spill out the door of the house. They weren't expecting me, but it wasn't like them to not come out to greet me.

I let myself in and followed the smell of cooking to the kitchen. What I saw froze me in the doorway. My father was seated, eyes closed, with his elbows on the table and his head propped up on a hand. He'd always been the strongest man in the room. I'd never seen him look so tired and . . . beaten down?

Fear lumped in my throat. Something was very, very wrong.

My attention flew to the tall man in jeans and a plaid shirt stirring a wooden spoon in a pot. When he turned I sucked in a breath. It was Cooper, but not how I remembered him. He was taller, more muscular, with the strong jaw of a grown man. When our eyes met there was a fire in his that sent a confusing heat washing through me.

I am so not over him.

He looked away as if he wasn't standing in my parents' kitchen and we could somehow pretend this wasn't happening. My attention returned to my father. "Dad?" I asked in a strangled voice.

My father's eyes flew open and he rose to his feet. "Amanda. What are you doing here?"

I rushed to stand beside him. "I was missing you and Mom. I thought I'd surprise you." I looked around then searched my father's face again. "Is something wrong?" Without answering, my father exchanged a look with Cooper. I began to panic. "Where is Mom?"

My father pressed his lips together in a line before answering. "She's resting."

"Is she fighting a cold?" I asked quickly.

He seemed to be struggling to look me in the eye. "She hasn't been feeling well lately."

"Have you spoken to the doctor?"

From behind me, Cooper said, "I've set the stew to simmer. I'll check the store then be home tonight if you need anything, Pete."

A swirl of anger filled me when he didn't so much as acknowledge me. I shot him a glare that said: *Go if you don't care enough to stay to make sure my family's okay.* Which didn't make a lot of sense since he'd obviously been cooking for my father so he did care about my family. *Just not me.*

My father nodded. "Thank you."

I'm being ridiculous. People take naps and my parents are getting older. I squared my shoulders. *And Cooper isn't the one who makes things awkward between us—I do that. I need to do better.* "Cooper." There, at least I'd said his name aloud.

He paused on his way to the door and turned. Our eyes met, but he broke the contact almost immediately. "It's good to see you, Amanda."

I stepped closer. There was something I felt had to be said, something that maybe I should have said a long time ago. "You don't have to leave because of me."

When his eyes raised to mine, the pain in his hit me like a sucker punch. "It's better if I go. You and your father have a lot to talk about."

"I blocked you in. Not on purpose." I cringed inwardly. *Way to sound stalkerish.* "I'll move my car."

He shook his head. "No need. I can walk. It's not that far."

I opened my mouth to say something more, but before I could, my father said, "Amanda, sit down. We do need to talk."

Time slowed and I forgot about Cooper. I sank onto one of the chairs and held my breath as my father took a seat as well. "What's wrong, Dad?"

The hand he laid over mine shook. "We should have told you, but we didn't want to worry you . . ."

The room spun and tilted. "What? What is it?"

"Your mother has cancer, baby. But she's beating it. She's strong." His eyes filled with tears that absolutely terrified me. My father didn't cry. "The treatments are cumulative. We were warned that the last few might be the hardest and this one has wiped her out. She's sleeping right now and we should let her have the peace of it."

"Cancer?" It couldn't be true. I couldn't not have known about it. No. "How long has she been getting treatments?"

"The doctors found the cancer in January. She started the treatments three months ago. We caught it early. And the prognosis is good."

His suffering was clear in the circles under his eyes and the weight he'd lost since I'd last seen him. Still, I had to ask, "Why didn't you tell me?"

His smile was sad. "We know how busy you are. We're so proud of you and everything you've accomplished. We're okay, Amanda. You just chose a tough weekend to come home."

I brought my hands up to my face and took a moment to absorb that it was real. I found myself expressing how I felt in a whisper. "I'm so sorry, Dad."

He leaned closer. "You have nothing to be sorry about, baby."

"I love you and Mom so much."

"We know you do."

I lowered my hands and looked him in the eye again. "Is Mom going to be okay?"

He pressed his lips together before answering. "If anyone is listening to my prayers she will be."

I stood, walked over to where he sat and wrapped my arms around him. "I wish I'd known, Dad. There is nothing I'm doing that is more important than what you're facing. We're stronger together."

He sniffed. "Someone raised you right."

I laughed and wiped a tear from my cheek. "Yeah, my parents are fucking amazing people."

When I straightened, he wagged a finger at me. "Watch your language, young lady."

I made my way over to the stove, filled a bowl with the

stew, then placed it in front of him. "I may swear a few more times. You just told me my mother has cancer." I sat heavily back onto a chair across from him.

He nodded toward the stove. "Cooper makes a good meat stew. Pour yourself a bowl."

"I don't eat when my stomach is churning."

He filled a spoon without lifting it to his mouth. "You get that from me. Cooper insists on staying until I have something though, and it actually makes me feel a little better. So go get a damn bowl."

My eyebrows rose. "Oh, who's swearing now?" That was also unlike my father, at least in front of his family.

"I just told my daughter my wife has cancer. Hang on. We could both do with a shot of whiskey."

He's drinking again? He'd struggled with alcohol after leaving the Army and credited my mother with helping him beat that demon. Seeing him rise to get the whiskey bottle showed me how close we were to losing my mother and how little everything else I'd thought was important actually was.

Relocating my business wouldn't be easy, but there was no other option in my head or my heart.

I'm moving home.

Chapter Four

Cooper

AFTER CHECKING ON the hardware store, I returned to my apartment above it and slammed my fist into the wall beside the door hard enough that I left a dent. *Stop. It doesn't matter.*

But it did.

Instead of staying at Pete's long enough to make sure everything was okay after he told Amanda about Dotty, I'd run. How anxious had I been to leave? I'd left my fucking truck in the driveway and walked home in the rain.

Why? Because I'd cultivated the art of turning off my emotions and the one person with the ability to tear through that defense and make me feel shit had just shown up—and nearly started crying in front of me.

I'd wanted to stay, hold her, promise her everything would be okay.

Me.

Eight years should have lessened my attraction to her, nullified the insane idea that I was meant to protect her. A memory came to me from the first time we'd met. I'd been in this very room—scared, angry, disgusted with myself and debating if I should leave that night or the next morning . . .

A knock on the door had startled me, filling me with the adrenaline needed to fight again if I had to. Pete had walked in with Amanda at his heels, both of them carrying plates of food for me. I've never forgotten the tears that filled her eyes as she looked at me.

I must have been a pitiful sight. Although I was tall, I'd never been athletic. Food had been scarce while I was on the run so I was thinner than normal, filthy and in clothes covered with dried blood. My face was still swollen from the beating I'd received from the last person who'd offered to help me.

"We brought you dinner," Pete had said in a gentle, but firm voice as Amanda had placed the food on a table that was dusty from lack of use.

Amanda had flashed a smile at me I hadn't returned. "And bedding. It's downstairs." She looked around. "We can help you make the bed and clean up a bit if you'd like."

I'd backed away from her as if repulsed because I was, not by her but myself. She was the proverbial girl next door in white tennis shoes, jean shorts with her long hair bouncing behind her in a ponytail—pure innocence.

I was a two-time killer with the blood of even her father still on the sleeve of my shirt. The only thing worse than meeting up with someone else who wanted to hurt me was coming face-to-face with someone who thought they could help me. I was too far gone. "No," I'd growled. "Stay away from me." She'd looked at her father. He'd nodded for her to leave and she had. I'd shot an angry look at Pete and declared, "I don't need anything from you. I don't even know why I'm still here."

"Whatever happened to you, son, you're safe now. Is there someone I can call? Parents? Family?"

"I'm eighteen," I lied. When I met his gaze again, I admitted, "And I have no one to go back to."

Pete had spoken slowly. "Then stay for a day. If it's not the most miserable one of your life, stay another. I could use help in the store and if you've got nowhere else to go, Driverton is as good a place as any to find your footing."

I'd shaken my head, "If you knew what I've done . . ."

"That's a conversation for another day, son. For now, get yourself cleaned up, fill that stomach of yours, and if you're still here in the morning come down and help stock the shelves."

"I tried to rob you."

"And I kicked your ass so we're even. What's your name?"

"Cooper," I'd said automatically, then snapped my teeth shut. When he waited for more, I glanced around and saw an author's name on the spine of a dust-covered book on the floor and decided to use it as my own. "Davis. Cooper Davis."

Ten years later I was still above the hardware store, still doing my best to avoid Pete's daughter, still tormented every time she was near. I didn't believe in fate, karma, a greater power, or life after death. The world was full of too much ugliness for any of it to be by design.

But there was something about Amanda that couldn't be explained or dismissed.

One look from her and I resented the power my past had over me. I didn't want to be the youngest son of a wealthy couple who'd died too soon to save their children from the evil circling them. I wanted to go back in time, do everything differently and meet her as someone who wouldn't be put in prison if my real identity was uncovered.

My hands fisted at my sides as I remembered the hurt expression in Amanda's eyes when I hadn't acknowledged her in her parents' kitchen. *Don't you see? I'm doing you a favor. Don't care about me. Go back to the city.*

I'd just changed into dry clothing when someone knocked on my door. I'd told Pete where I'd be if he needed me. He wouldn't leave Dotty's side unless something had happened. I rushed to the door and threw it open.

Amanda.

I swayed back onto my heels as she pushed past me into the room. "I know I'm not your favorite person, but I'm going crazy." Her hair was damp from the rain and she sounded flustered, but when she spun and faced me the effect of her full attention on me made it difficult to breathe. "Are my parents okay? I saw my mother and she told me things aren't as bad as they look. She said her prognosis is good. I need to know the truth. How bad is her cancer?"

I let out a slow breath and closed the door behind me but held on to the doorknob. "I only know what they tell me."

She took a step closer. "And what is that? Cooper, it's killing me that I missed something this big. Give it to me straight." Her eyes were a little puffy and her nose was red but, God, she was beautiful. "Please."

I cleared my throat. "The treatments are hard on your mother. The doctors are cautiously optimistic. Dotty has another treatment scheduled in a month and more testing. The cancer was spreading aggressively so there's a chance this is only the beginning of a long battle."

Eyes flashing, Amanda stepped closer still. "You should have told me."

There was a lot I should have done when it came to her. I should have kept my hands off her the night of the prom. I should have left town after she did. "Your father didn't want—"

"Sometimes it's not about what someone *wants*, it's about what's right."

I sucked in a breath. *Exactly. That's my mantra when it comes to you.* In place of what I couldn't say aloud, I lifted and lowered my shoulders. When she looked as if she wanted to say more, I said, "Is that all you wanted?"

I wanted her to say yes and go.

I wanted her to stay.

See, that's what she does to me. I can't think straight around her.

Her head tilted to the side. "No, there's something else I need to say . . ."

I held her gaze but said nothing.

Wrapping her arms protectively around herself. "I'm sorry if I ever made you feel that I don't like you, Cooper. I'm grateful for all you've done for my parents . . . especially recently."

Had I let myself feel anything in response I might have been overwhelmed. There was a yearning in her eyes that drew me in. I needed to get her out of my apartment before I said or did anything I'd regret.

She lowered her arms and continued, "I know you've been through some rough times and—"

"You. Don't. Know. Me." There. That had to be clear enough. *Go, Amanda. For God's sake. Go.*

The compassion in her expression reminded me of the first time we'd met, confusing me even more. I'd done my best to distance myself from back then, but that didn't change who I was or what I'd done. Her voice was gentle. "I do. My parents were telling me how you've been there for them and I wasn't surprised. You've always been good to them. When you left tonight, I didn't want it to be because you thought I didn't want you there."

When she stepped closer, I released the doorknob and sidestepped. "Go home, Amanda."

She blinked a few times quickly and her face crumbled. "I'm sorry, you're right, I shouldn't be here." She didn't make a move to leave.

I swallowed hard.

She sniffed. "After my parents went to bed, I sat there thinking about the possibility that my mother could have died without me ever knowing she was ill and it freaked me out. I had to get out of there and find someone I could talk to."

And she'd come to me. She had no idea how much I wished I was what she needed. I wasn't. "Don't you have . . . friends?" It was a dick thing to ask, but it was better than suggesting she call one of the men she was fucking.

She looked away, bit her bottom lip, then met my gaze

again; the pain in her eyes gutted me. "Not really." She paused then added, "No one I could talk to about this. Have you ever looked around and realized, despite your life being full of people, you're still alone?"

"Yes," I said in a harsher tone than I'd meant to. I knew that feeling all too well.

"I was okay until I saw my mother." She wiped at the corner of one of her eyes. "I know people get sick. I know no one lives forever, but my mother has to be okay. This can't be happening." She took a deep breath. "I'm scared. This might sound crazy, but when we were younger knowing you were around always made me feel like nothing bad could happen . . ."

Fuck.

Her eyes searched mine as she added, "That's how I want to feel tonight."

Tears began to stream down her cheeks and I pulled her into my arms, tucking her against my chest. I didn't tell her everything would be okay. I had no idea if it would be, but I held her. Loss was something I understood far too well.

She wept for what felt like an eternity then raised her face and it was as if no time had gone by at all since we'd danced at her prom. My cock swelled in anticipation. The world around us faded away. I was a tangle of emotion and need. My mouth hovered above hers as the last of my restraint teetered. "Amanda, I'm no hero. If you keep looking at me like that, I'm going to kiss you."

She brought a hand up to cup one side of my face. "Would that be so bad?"

How could it be when holding her had me feeling more alive than I'd felt . . . maybe ever. She'd come to me. I might not be able to give her a relationship or even the truth about who I was, but I could love her.

All night.

With every fiber of my being.

Chapter Five

Amanda

*H*E WANTS ME. Evidence that the feeling was mutual was hard and throbbing against my stomach. I ran my hand up his strong back and arched against him. I'd always considered myself an independent woman, but that night I wanted the kind of comfort only he could offer me.

Talking to my parents, learning how bad things had been for them, had left me shattered on the inside. Hearing how Cooper had cared for them sent my emotions into overload. I'd had to thank him, had to hear from him if things were worse than my parents implied.

Rational or not, I trusted Cooper on a level I didn't trust other men. And that night I needed his strength, his touch. My body was humming as I waited for his kiss.

He brought his hands around to cup my face. When his mouth claimed mine, it was with a tenderness that almost had me crying again. I expected a roughness that never came. He was so controlled, so careful.

Too careful to be what I needed that night.

We were both breathing heavily when he raised his head.

He ran his hands down my arms gently. "You've been drinking."

"Just one shot." My voice was breathy and reflected exactly how turned on I was.

"You should go."

I swayed and blinked a few times. "Why?"

My only comfort was he looked as tormented by his suggestion as I was. "I want to kiss away your sadness, but if you stay, we're going to fuck."

His raw desire sent a flutter through my stomach. There was no thought of where this would or wouldn't lead us. It was primal, heady . . .

I wrapped my arms around his neck, pulled his mouth down to mine and let my kiss tell him what I wanted. He groaned and gathered me closer.

His earlier restraint fell away and his hunger for me flamed my own desire. I writhed against him, loving how every inch of me felt against the hard warmth of him. His hands gripped my hips and I moaned as he moved me back and forth over his excitement.

He raised his head again, but this time there was only fire in his eyes. His hands slipped beneath the hem of my shirt and I lifted my arms to allow him to pull it up and over my head. He unsnapped my bra and I tossed it to the floor.

Not one to be passive, I hastily relieved him of his shirt as well. Our next kiss was gloriously skin to skin. His hands ran up my bare back. I explored his torso with rough hands. As we kissed deeply, he reached between us, unbuttoned my jeans, then slid them and my panties down slowly. We broke off the kiss long enough for me to kick out of my jeans and shoes then I turned my attention to stripping the rest of his clothing off as well.

We stood there for a moment taking each other in. He was sheer male perfection. Tall, muscled, just a little wild. I should have felt vulnerable, but this was Cooper and this was how I'd always ached for him to look at me.

His huge cock waved in the air between us, leaving no doubt of what he wanted, but something beyond passion darkened his eyes. I reached out and took one of his hands in mine. "Cooper?"

His expression was tight. "You're Pete's daughter."

"I am, but I'm also an adult."

He lifted a hand and ran the back of it across one of my cheeks. "I don't want to disappoint you."

"Oh." I glanced down at his hard shaft then met his gaze again. Did it not maintain? Some men had issues. I hadn't been with one like that yet, but I could imagine how difficult it would be for a man to admit.

I quickly asked myself if that would be a game changer for wanting to be with him. Was I there just for the fuck?

No. I want more than that from Cooper. I always have.

I swallowed hard. "Is there something I can do that would help?"

"Help?" He looked lost for a moment, then a twinkle entered his eyes. "Sure."

I ran my hands over his flat stomach to encircle his cock. It was exciting to take charge as this was a novel experience for me. I was used to the man always taking the lead, which sometimes led to me faking my level of pleasure. "What do you like?"

His face flushed. "Anything you want to do."

My body began to hum with anticipation. I began to stroke my hands up and down his cock. "You're a very trusting soul."

He sucked in a breath then shook his head. "Only when it comes to you."

I continued the caress then leaned forward and kissed his collarbone. "I like that." I kissed my way down his chest then sank to my knees. His eyes closed when I took him into my mouth. Nothing about the throbbing hardness of him hinted at an issue, but I wasn't in the mental state to ask questions. I loved the taste of him, the feel of him, the promise of his size.

Moving up and down, I took him deeper. He dug his hands into my hair forcefully, just shy of painfully. I used every little trick I'd learned along the way to increase his pleasure and reveled in the power of it. I flicked my tongue over his tip, swirled it around, took him in and slid him out.

When he tensed and I thought he might come in my mouth, he withdrew and pulled me to my feet. Had I done something wrong? Was he someone who required speed? I hoped not.

As if I weighed nothing he lifted me into his arms and strode across the room to his bed. I bounced once as he tossed me onto it then caught my breath as he settled himself between my legs.

We kissed and I spread my legs for him. The tip of his

cock grazed my wet center. I dug my hands into his shoulders and nearly begged him to take me, but his tongue circling mine prevented me from doing more than emitting sounds of need.

I nearly cried when he broke off the kiss and began to kiss his way down my neck. There was no patience in me, but he took his time loving each of my breasts slowly. Lightly nipping, teasing, driving me out of my mind.

Ever so slowly, he moved down my body, caressing, claiming, leaving no area untouched. When his face hovered over my sex, he parted my folds, and let his hot breath warm me. I gripped the bedsheets on either side of me and swore.

He ran his tongue lightly over me, circling but not giving me what I craved. I opened wider, started swearing softly, and jutted up against his mouth. In response he dove in, swirling his tongue in mind-erasing ways.

His fingers dipped within me and pumped while he worked my clit in the most magical way. I called out his name when I came and was still shuddering from the pleasure of it when he rose above me then drove his cock deep inside.

All gentleness was gone. I was clinging to him while he pounded into me. He was so big, almost too big, but in the most delicious way. I was floating between my last orgasm and another one rising within me.

He was powerful—relentless. Deeper. Harder. Faster. I gave myself over to the wild ride and just when I thought I might come for a second time he pulled out and flipped me over. After pulling me up to my knees, he entered me from behind and fucked me so hard I fell forward. He wrapped an arm around my hips, hauled me back up and continued to pound away.

I came for the second time with a whimper and clenched my sex around his cock. And still he thrust into me. In and out, so deep and wonderful I shuddered from the pleasure of being fucked right through an orgasm.

When he finally came it was with a final thrust and a growl of my name. We rolled together onto the bed, side by side. For a long time neither of us spoke, the only sound in the room was our ragged breathing coming back to normal.

A thought occurred to me that I spontaneously asked, "You don't have an issue, do you?"

"No, ma'am." He scooped an arm under me and pulled me to his side then gave the side of my head a kiss. "But I don't know a man who'd turn down an offer of help."

I wrinkled my nose up at him but smiled then settled my head against his chest listening to his heartbeat. Being with him felt too good to have been a mistake. "Cooper?"

He rolled onto his back but kept one arm around me. "Mmm?"

"What's your favorite food?"

He ran a hand down my back in a caress. "That's what you want to know about me?"

I went up onto one elbow and looked down at him. "I'd like to know anything and everything you'd like to tell me."

His chest expanded as he took in a deep breath. When his eyes met mine, they were burning with an emotion I didn't understand. "Don't."

I shook my head in confusion. "Don't what?"

"I care about you, Amanda . . ."

That was a relief to hear . . . except . . . "But?"

He gave me a long look, then tumbled me down into his arms again. "Nothing that matters tonight. Do you feel any better?"

It was an odd question, like what we'd shared had been medicinal. I did a quick self-assessment and realized I did feel much calmer. "I do, actually."

"Good." He kissed my forehead then closed his eyes.

It didn't feel right to have shared so much and so little. "You didn't answer my question."

Without opening his eyes, he said, "Pizza. I never had it before I came to Driverton and I love it."

"You never had pizza before you came here? How's that even possible?"

He shook his head once. "Go to sleep, Amanda, or go home."

I lay there next to him, thinking about how rude he was, but that didn't stop me from loving the strength of his arms around me. I wanted to say something snarky in return or demand that he apologize, but instead I yawned, decided I'd do both in the morning and fell asleep.

Chapter Six

Cooper

I KEPT MY eyes shut until Amanda's breathing deepened and I was certain she was asleep. In my teen years being near her had caused a physical ache that sex with other women hadn't alleviated. Holding her in my arms in my bed, with the taste of her still on my lips while knowing we could never have more, filled me with a different kind of ache.

I shouldn't have had sex with her, but my life was full of regret for things I shouldn't have done—things nothing I did could make up for. I'd been young but that excuse only carries a person so far. That's what I told every runaway who thought nothing they did could make a difference.

Life is full of choices that define us.

I could have believed my brother, done something to protect my sister, stayed and fought instead of run. I was young, gullible, and unaware of how ugly the world could be . . .

I sighed.

Excuses are like assholes, they have no ability to make shit more appealing.

Amanda snuggled closer to my side and I turned so I could soak in her beauty. It didn't surprise me that she'd decided to move back to Driverton after learning about her mother's cancer. Amanda had always taken care of those around her: stray animals, friends, neighbors . . . not me, though. I'd never allowed that.

Gently, I traced the side of her face and frowned. Hurt and alone, she'd come to me. As much as I hated that I couldn't be part of her life, I wanted her to have a full one away from Driverton. I imagined her with a large circle of friends and more potential dates than she had time for. But when she hadn't felt safe she'd come to me . . .

I wanted to wake her and promise her she'd never be alone again, but that wasn't where this was going. I couldn't be the friend she needed or the strong shoulder she was yearning for.

I really shouldn't have fucked her.

No matter how good it was.

No matter how much I'd love to wake her and do it again.

She stirred in my arms. "Cooper?"

Shit. I closed my eyes again.

"I know you're awake," she persisted.

I groaned. "I'm not."

She chided softly, "Oh, sorry. You're obviously sound asleep."

I opened my eyes and turned to face her. God, a man could happily spend a lifetime lost in those eyes of hers. So open. So trusting. How did she not have someone to call her own?

She laid a hand on my chest. "What are you thinking?"

I tensed. There was nothing in my head she'd want to hear. "That's every man's least favorite question."

She wrinkled her nose. "Then you don't know a lot of men. I've found that many love talking about themselves."

I didn't have a response to that. I didn't like the idea of her with other men, but I knew I had no right to feel or express that so I simply looked back at her.

Her expression turned more serious. "How is it possible to feel so close to you and also like I don't know you at all?"

I could have told her that was not only deliberate but for the best, however that wasn't what she needed to hear. She'd come to me to be comforted and if that was all I had to offer her, I could at least do that well. I kissed her briefly, gently. "I'm not an easy person to get to know."

She blinked slowly. "Understatement of the year."

"But that doesn't mean I don't care."

"I know," she said softly. "That's why I'm here."

I let out a breath. "You shouldn't be."

Neither of us spoke for a moment and she frowned. "You don't have to worry. I understand that sex is sometimes just sex."

Yeah. That tore through me and left me speechless. Was I supposed to declare that it had meant something to me and open the door to her getting hopeful and hurt? Or agree and pretend this night wouldn't stay with me until my last breath? There was no right answer.

After a prolonged silence, she asked, "Should I go?"

It was the kind of question a one-night stand might ask

and it gutted me. If miracles were possible, if I could have shed everything I hated about myself, I would have for her. My faith in miracles had departed a long time ago, along with my ability to imagine my life as anything but what it was. I choked out one word. "Stay."

She searched my face for a long time, then settled her head on my chest again. "I don't regret coming here. I needed this."

I kissed the top of her head and simply held her.

I didn't.

I'd been comfortably numb before she'd returned home. I didn't want to feel anything, but I was damn near blinking back tears. What the hell was wrong with me?

When she lifted her head to look at me, I kissed her. There was so much I couldn't put to words, but I could show her. I took my time and loved every inch of her over and over. Afterward, limbs still intertwined with hers, I joined her in a sated slumber.

I was woken too soon by a knock on the door of my apartment. I threw on pants, tucked a blanket over Amanda, and rushed to answer the door before she roused as well. Just before opening the door I thought, *God don't let it be Pete.*

It was Tom. He took one look at me then at the outline of a body beneath the blanket on my bed and said, "I'll wait for you downstairs. We have a job."

I nodded once, closed the door then crossed the room to stand over Amanda. Leaving while she slept felt wrong, but there was no way the morning wasn't going to be awkwardly painful. Not being there, giving her a reason to be angry with me, was probably for the best.

I considered writing her a note then rolled my eyes when I imagined what it might say:

Amanda,

Last night was great.

Let's not do it again,
Cooper

Yeah, it was probably better to just go. I finished dressing then headed downstairs to meet Sheriff Tom. We didn't speak until we were in his cruiser and he handed me a file. "Sorry to break up your night," he said.

I opened the file as I spoke. "It's morning anyway." Reading the notes brought me both calm and purpose. This was who I was. This was my purpose. Amanda might be disappointed when she woke without me, but she'd get over it.

Shawn Roy, a fourteen-year-old boy had disappeared from a nearby city. The file didn't contain much information. He'd been missing for over a week. His phone had been recovered thirty miles outside city limits. That wasn't good.

Tom cleared his throat. "Is that Amanda's car?"

Without looking up from the file, I asked, "Did you bring a burner phone?"

"Of course," he handed it to me along with an envelope. "No payment expected from this one. Mother works two jobs to pay rent. The local PD wrote this off as gang related."

"Gang?" I scanned the statement. "Was he in one?

There's nothing in the statement that implies he was." I exchanged a look with Tom then expelled a breath in disgust. "Got it."

"I feel the same, but we're making changes, Cooper," Tom said. "Bring me the evidence and I'll get it in the hands of the right people. Those who didn't bother to investigate will be reprimanded. I'll make sure of it."

For a small-town sheriff, Tom had a network of powerful friends he'd made through our endeavors. I had no doubt he'd follow through on that promise. My face tightened. "Over a week is a long time to be missing. This might be a recovery." *God, I hate those.*

"Either way, let's bring him home with enough to nail the perp who did this to him."

"You already have a lead?" I closed the file, pocketed the phone and envelope.

"Just what my gut tells me. A male neighbor has been harassing the mother. She filed a restraining order on him but there wasn't enough to make it stick. According to her, Shawn threatened to confront the neighbor himself, then never came home from school."

"That's not in the file."

"Doesn't fit the gang narrative, does it?"

"Right."

"And the neighbor?"

"He says Shawn never went to see him."

"Any video? Evidence that Shawn's cell was in that location?"

"Neither."

"What do we have for resources for this one?"

"Depends how deep this goes or what the mother decides. Keep your hands clean because I want to shine a bright light on how this should have been handled better."

"Always do." I ran a hand over my forehead. "Assuming I find the kid alive, that family needs relocation."

"That's your part. I can't be officially in this one, not if we're going to bring anyone down."

Tom had loyalty to his badge, but no loyalty to those who betrayed it. I understood that. "Ideally, when I return with Shawn, she'll agree to move away with him. If so, I'll need funds to set her up in a new place as well as some leads for employment for her."

"I'll start lining that up, but if her son is . . . she may be in no condition to do much of anything."

"We'll worry about that later. For now, move a generous amount over. This family needs help."

"Will do." My hand was on the door handle when Tom said, "Be careful, Cooper. The neighbor has a long rap sheet and nothing to lose. Don't get yourself killed."

"I should be so lucky," I muttered. When his eyebrows rose, I forced a smile. "Don't worry, the good die young . . . so I'm here for the long haul."

He nodded toward Amanda's car. "How's Dotty?"

"Tired. No answers on the testing yet. Check in on her and Pete while I'm gone, will you? Pete is taking this hard."

"Absolutely."

"Oh, and Ollie's roof needs to be redone. Shit I was going to get that done this weekend for him. I've ordered the supplies. Everette and Levi were supposed to help me out."

"We'll get it done. My brother's in town. He'll do it for free beer." After a pause, he asked, "Does Amanda know anything?"

"No."

"Where did you tell her you're going?"

I glanced up at the window of my room above the store. "I didn't."

Tom let out a whistle. "You're just leaving? That won't go over well."

"Doesn't matter." This job couldn't have come at a better time. It was a concrete reminder of all the reasons I had no business having feelings for Amanda. From outside of the car I said, "I'll contact you when I've found Shawn."

File tucked under one arm, I made my way back to where my truck was still parked. I thought I'd successfully gotten into my vehicle and started it up without waking Pete, but he appeared at the door.

I lowered the driver's window. We exchanged a long look that only a father and a man who'd just slept with his daughter could. He didn't have to say a word, everything was right there in his eyes.

He looked from me to the empty passenger seat.

I motioned with my head in the direction of my place.

He walked down the steps, came to stand at my door, and searched my face. "You're leaving."

I nodded once.

"Usual reason?"

"Fourteen-year-old boy. Missing for over a week."

"You think he's still alive?"

"No way to know."

"Good luck." Pete inhaled sharply. "How much does Amanda know?"

"Nothing. It's better that way."

"Is it? She'll be hurt when she learns you left."

I swallowed hard and held his gaze as I said, "Pete, you and I both know I'm not the man for your daughter."

"Then this is where you tell me she wasn't with you last night."

I couldn't, so I didn't.

His face tightened and he straightened. "Cooper, I love you like a son, but when it comes to Amanda . . ."

He didn't have to finish. I understood. My time in Driverton was quickly coming to an end. When Amanda returned for good it would be my turn to leave. "This job is complicated. I may be gone a week. Maybe longer. Everette should be able to cover for me at the store." I didn't say long term, but I had a feeling Pete heard it anyway.

He didn't say that wouldn't be necessary. "Be careful, Cooper."

"I always am." I put the truck in reverse, but paused before backing up. "I'm sorry, Pete."

He stepped back from the truck. "I'm not happy with you, but we all saw this coming. She's always had a sweet spot in her heart for you."

Rather than attempting to respond to that, I pressed the gas and put distance between me and everything I didn't want to think about. I'd become comfortable in Driverton—

too comfortable. I'd forgotten that nothing good was forever.

Luckily the world was full of horrible people who did heinous things to each other. I'd find another town, another source of "jobs."

Life would go on.

Chapter Seven

Amanda

I WOKE IN stages. First, I stretched and smiled, marveling at how deeply I'd slept and how good that felt. As I became aware that I wasn't in my own bed adrenaline rushed in and I sat straight up in a rush.

Sunlight streamed in through the windows. I gathered a sheet to cover my nakedness then realized I was alone . . . in Cooper's room above the hardware store. I groaned as I remembered what had brought me there.

My parents would be awake already. The last thing I wanted to do was worry either of them on top of everything else they had going on. Spotting my cell phone near the bed, I leaned over to retrieve it and sent a text to my father: **Sorry I didn't tell you I was going to sleep out. Would you like me to pick up anything on my way back?**

It wasn't the ideal thing to text, but better than not acknowledging that they might have worried when they'd woken and I was gone. **I told your mother you went out to do a little shopping for us so pick up some yogurt, bread, and some muffins.**

My hands shook as I read the message. I had *the best* parents. It wasn't that we didn't make mistakes or ever annoy each other, but the backbone of our relationship was that we wanted the best for each other. I'd tell Mom, but I was relieved my father hadn't let her worry about me. She needed all of her strength to heal.

Thanks, Dad. I'll be home in a few.

Sitting on the edge of Cooper's bed, I relived every word, every touch. It had all felt so right. I told myself it shouldn't. I should be filled with regret or embarrassment. I wasn't.

Cooper had feelings for me. Proof of that had been in the tenderness of his kisses and the way he held me like he never wanted to let me go. He might be worried that having any kind of relationship with me might affect his standing with my parents, but we could work around that.

I understood how grateful Cooper was to my father and it was part of what I loved about both of them. I stood abruptly.

No. Don't do that. Don't put more meaning on what we did.

My heart was thudding wildly in my chest as I gathered my clothing off the floor. I couldn't forget the amount of emotion when he'd told me to stay. I wasn't reading into how he felt. Cooper and I had always had a connection.

I'd done everything I could to forget him. I'd moved away. I'd told myself and everyone I met he'd never meant anything to me. As I dressed I made a face as I remembered how many of the men I'd dated had asked me to stop saying Cooper's name.

No wonder half the town was waiting for us to wake up

and become a couple. By his own admission, Cooper wasn't an easy man to get to know, but that made our connection that much more.

Fully dressed again, I walked around looking for . . . something . . . a clue regarding where he was . . . a hint that he might feel the same way I did.

No television.

No technology.

Shelves overflowing with books of all genres—ancient classics to modern mysteries. The breadth of his reading interest was surprising and not at the same time. He'd learned a lot from my father, but then continued educating himself on countless useful skills. He could fix a person's toilet as easily as he could figure out why their garden had stopped producing. The way he helped everyone was a common topic whenever I came home. Cooper might not have been born in Driverton, but no one would know that if they spoke to any of the residents.

He's more loved here than I am.

The thought made me smile. Even if that were true, I was happy for him. Regardless of what had brought him to our town, he'd earned the faith everyone had in him. Was it any wonder I hadn't found a man who compared? How could I be attracted to men who bragged endlessly about how wonderful they were, when Cooper was wonderful without ever saying a word about it? I looked around his space and sighed.

Of course I'd hoped he'd still be there when I woke, but knowing Cooper he was probably getting a coffee and donut for me at Manju's across the street. He'd always known how to make me smile.

I slept with Cooper. It still didn't feel real. I didn't want to get too excited about it, but this didn't feel like a mistake . . . it felt like the beginning of something amazing.

I walked over to the window and looked out onto the street below. *It's happening.*

My determination to wait for Cooper waned the longer he didn't return. After an hour, I decided he must have slipped away to help someone. He didn't have a cell phone so he had no way of calling me.

Although I have a cell phone and he could borrow someone else's.

I told myself I was getting worked up about nothing.

Still, a note would have been nice.

Something.

I left his place and did a quick shop for my parents before heading home. When I pulled into my parents' driveway I noticed Cooper's truck was gone. My father rose from a chair on the porch and came down to my car to help me carry in the groceries.

I handed him a grocery bag and tried to sound nonchalant as I asked, "Cooper picked up his truck?"

"He did."

I gathered up the other bag of groceries and closed the door of my car. "Did he say where he was going?"

"Let's talk inside, Amanda."

That didn't sound good. Of all the things I'd imagined, I hadn't considered that something might be wrong. "Is he okay? Did something happen?"

My father adjusted the bag of groceries in his arms. "He's gone, Amanda. He left town."

I swayed on my feet. "I don't understand. What do you mean he left town?"

"He might not be back for weeks."

No. That didn't make any sense. "Where did he go?"

"An out-of-town job."

I shook my head. "He works for you. Did you send him somewhere?" I couldn't imagine my father doing that, no matter how he felt about us being together. Beyond anything else, my father had always respected my right to make my own mistakes.

"I didn't send him anywhere."

"Did you know he was leaving today?"

"No."

I gripped the bag of food so tightly one of the packages in it made a crunching sound. "I thought he helped you and Mom out. You've always said he's so reliable. How reliable can he be if he up and leaves with no notice?"

Leaves them.

Leaves me.

I didn't want to believe it.

"He has his reasons," my father said firmly.

"Not good enough," I ground out.

"I know, baby. I know."

He did and that just made things worse. "He wouldn't just leave without even saying good-bye to me."

"This is what he does." When my father's gaze fell away I

knew exactly what Cooper had done. He'd taken the time to tell my father that he was leaving town, but me? Of course not.

How many times do I need to make a fool of myself over him before I understand he does not return my feelings? "I'm such an idiot."

I didn't realize I'd said the words aloud until my father responded with, "No, you're not. Cooper can't get out of his own damn way long enough to see that he's not the boy I caught trying to rob our store. I swear that's why he takes these jobs. He thinks it's the only way he can repent."

That was a lot of guilt to carry around for a failed robbery. "*These jobs?* What jobs?"

"I've already said more than I should have, Amanda. Just know that he has another side to him and that's why he feels he can't be with you."

"That doesn't make any sense. What other side of him? Where did he go?" Shaking my head, I squeezed the bag even tighter. "Does he have a wife or something in another town? Is that what you're trying to tell me?"

"I would tell you if that were the case." My father made a pained face. "He's broken, Amanda. Maybe too broken for any of us to help."

"I don't know what that means."

My father cleared his throat. "Ask him to explain if you see him again."

"If?" A cold settled on me. "Did you tell him to stay away from me?"

"I didn't need to say it."

"Dad—"

"He's not the one, Amanda. If he was, he wouldn't leave you."

The contents of the bag I'd been holding crashed to the ground at my feet. A glass bottle of pizza sauce shattered spraying its contents in a red mess in every direction.

Perhaps it was the shock of it, but I laughed.

And then I started to cry.

My father put down his bag, pulled me to his chest for a hug and rocked back and forth. "I'm sorry, Amanda. Sometimes life sucks."

It did. It really did.

"I'm not even a crier," I said angrily as tears ran down my face.

"Me neither, but sometimes you've got to let it out."

I raised my head and sniffed. Shame slammed in. "I'm so sorry, Dad. Here I am going on and on about something stupid when you and Mom have been dealing with something serious."

He held me back from him and smiled at me with emotion shining in his eyes. "Pain isn't a competitive sport. We're all just doing the best we can." His hands dropped away. "What do you say we have another shot of whiskey?"

There wasn't much I could do about my mother's cancer or Cooper's disappearance, but it might be time to address my father's choice of a crutch. "Before breakfast?"

He shrugged. "It takes the edge off."

I remembered stories my mother told me about how much peace my father found in nature. "You know what I'd like more than that? Remember how we used to go for a walk down to the river and skip rocks before school? You told me it would help me focus better in math."

He chuckled. "I made that up. Getting you out of the house before school gave your mother some quiet time before she headed over to the store."

I smiled even as I shook my head. "Well, it worked. So come on, we're going for a walk and to see if you're still better at skipping stones."

He straightened. "I'm sure I am."

"I don't know. You're getting old. You'll have to prove it."

After putting the bags of food on the porch and cleaning up the spilled sauce, we walked without speaking for a few minutes, then my father said, "It's been hard, Amanda."

"I know, Dad. But I have a job that I can do from anywhere and I'm going to move home to help out."

He didn't tell me I shouldn't or that he didn't need the help.

We both knew it was the right move.

No matter what Cooper felt for me or wherever the hell he ran off to hide, my father was right: Cooper couldn't be the man for me.

If he was, he'd be here.

Chapter Eight

Cooper

THREE WEEKS LATER, I arrived back in Driverton late enough that the roads were empty and the streetlights were on. After parking my truck behind the hardware store, I tiredly made my way up to my room above it, let myself in, and kicked off my boots before slamming the door behind me.

It had been weeks since I'd been home—if I could call a bed and four walls anything but the place I sleep. Although finding Shawn had taken longer than expected, I'll admit that I'd taken my time returning to Driverton.

Shawn was alive, though, and with his mother again. That was what mattered the most. His mother had refused to bring charges against the neighbor who'd taken her son, beaten him, and left him for dead in the woods. She was afraid and I couldn't blame her. No matter what I said or what police might promise her, bad things happened to good people.

And often bad people got away with far too much before they were stopped.

She'd also feared retribution from the police as well if their shortcomings in the case were made public. I couldn't assure her that was an impossibility. Life wasn't fair and I had limited clout to address that.

It hadn't felt right to leave the neighbor free while relocating Shawn and his mother to South Carolina where she had some family. Doing anything else, though, would have gone against my agreement with Tom to contain our work to retrieval and not dabble in punishment or execution. No matter how bad things got, no matter what we witnessed, we pulled each other back from the edge when we teetered.

This one had been tough for me. If Tom hadn't sworn he'd make sure the neighbor found justice through the legal system, even if it took time to prosecute him on something else, I don't know that I could have walked away.

It was still hard to believe Shawn had survived. He hadn't been strong enough to make it to a major road, but he'd found a cabin and hunkered down in it, hoping his injuries would heal enough for him to leave it . . . or that someone would find him. Nearly three weeks without much more than water from a well to live on, the kid had been in rough shape by the time I tracked him to the cabin.

I stripped down and headed toward my shower. The hot spray did nothing to improve my mood. Life was so fucking confusing. I didn't believe in luck, but when I thought about all the ways my search for him could have failed, it was tempting to believe in something.

My search for Shawn had started where his phone had been found, then I worked my way back from there. I'd spent days chasing potential leads without success. I must have spoken to everyone within a ten-mile radius until I found someone who thought he'd seen a man in a blue sedan driving down one of the backroads.

The neighbor had a blue sedan. That should have been helpful.

I'd driven every backroad and talked to countless people in the small town that abutted a large forested area. No one remembered seeing the car. I spoke to so many that some greeted me by name when I approached them. Yet, nothing.

I'd stopped for coffee and gas at a store where I'd already interviewed everyone when a young hiker walked in and asked for a map of the forest. He said he and his friends were looking to camp somewhere remote and jokingly asked if there was an abandoned cabin anywhere in the area where they could party.

The clerk had laughed the idea off but, after the hiker had left, told me there was one that he and his friends had made an ATV trail to, but he wasn't sharing that spot.

I asked him how long it'd been since he'd been to it. When he'd said about a month because things at school had been so busy, I handed him a hundred-dollar bill and he gave me directions to it.

I couldn't say how I'd known Shawn would be there, but I was certain that was where I'd find him. And I did.

If I hadn't stopped for coffee . . .

If the hiker hadn't asked about a cabin . . .

There were times when it almost felt as if I were receiving a little extra help when it came to finding these kids. How did that make any sense? If there was any rhyme or reason to the universe, Shawn wouldn't have been taken in the first place.

After a long shower I toweled off and fell into bed without bothering with boxers. It was a warm evening and I normally would have opened a window, but I was exhausted. Sleep should have come quickly, but of course it didn't— that would have been a gift.

Instead I lay there wondering how long it had taken Amanda to get over me. Had it been instant? She woke up, found out I was gone and—bam—everything she felt for me died?

Had she hung on longer? Waited for me to return? Cried when I didn't?

I rolled over and punched my pillow. I could live with the first scenario. It was hard to stomach the second. I wished I could tell her there'd never been anyone in my heart but her—and there never would be.

It probably would have been better for everyone if I'd simply not returned to Driverton, but I wanted to check in on Dotty one last time, return Pete's tools, and maybe get a glimpse of Amanda . . . even if that would be its own kind of torture.

I wanted one more beer at Ollie's, to taste one more slice of Mrs. Williams's pie, a chance to remind Everette to shovel out Old Man Burrow's chicken coop since I wouldn't be around to do that anymore. I needed to tell Levi to find a real mechanic for his farm machinery. Or ask Pete to teach him the basics as he'd done with me.

I rolled over again and groaned. I didn't have more than a suitcase of things worth packing. It shouldn't have been so hard to leave. I'd known this day would come. I'd imagined it would be because my identity had been discovered and I'd need to run before being charged with my uncle's murder. I never thought it would be because I'd hurt Amanda.

I closed my eyes and made a mental checklist of all the things I needed to do before leaving for good. It could all be done in one day. *This might be my last night in this bed . . . in this town.*

There was a certain amount of irony to being as miserable on my last night there as I had been on my first.

If I do have a guardian angel, I'd like to file a formal complaint on him: He sucks.

That brought a slight smile to my lips. *Sorry, not sorry. He does.*

I'm requesting an immediate upgrade.

No one answered me. Nothing happened.

And I wasn't surprised at all.

Chapter Nine

Amanda

Present Day

I WOKE IN my childhood bed to a knock on the door. I'd arrived the night before, been disappointed to hear that Cooper was still out of town, and had decided to spend the night. How could no one know where he was? Why did it seem like people were protecting him?

From me? This was my town too.

I sat up in my bed and said, "Come in."

Looking a thousand times better than she had a few weeks earlier, my mother handed me a steaming cup of tea and took a seat on the edge of my bed. "So, guess whose truck is parked at the hardware store?"

My hands shook, nearly spilling the hot liquid. "Cooper's?"

"He got in late last night. Everette told Ollie who told his mother who called me."

That sounded about right. "Good. I need to talk to him."

Attempting to look casually interested in the answer, my

mother asked, "About anything in particular?"

I glanced down at the tea, wondered why she would have chosen that instead of coffee, then met my mother's gaze again. "You know, don't you?"

Her smile was gentle. "I wasn't sure until just now, but I used to get bloody noses when I was pregnant with you. When I saw you with one last week, I had a feeling."

"Does Dad know?"

"I didn't say anything to him. He's been so happy having you around more. I doubt he's thinking about much past that."

I put the tea aside and took her hand in mine. "His improved mood has more to do with your good news than my visits, but I do love spending more time with you both."

Her smile widened. "He said the same when I told him how happy you look here. You're two peas in a pod, do you know that?"

I smiled. "I am happier here." My hand went to my stomach and my expression turned more serious. "At least I was. Things are about to change, Mom, whether I'm ready for them to or not."

"You're ready. You have an income, a roof over your head, and a family who loves you."

I blinked back tears and bent forward to hug her. "Thank you, Mom. I know I'll be okay. It's just scary."

She sat back and nodded. "Life is scary, but I wouldn't want to miss a moment of it."

Even at her weakest, my mother's spirit had remained strong. She inspired me to rise rather than fall in the face of adversity. Still, something else had to be said. "I'm sorry this is happening now, Mom. You already have so much on your plate—"

"Are you kidding? My first grandchild is on the way and my baby just moved home which means I won't miss a moment of that miracle. I'll admit my final round of chemo was rough, but I'm feeling stronger every day and the tests are all saying I'm clear. You've given me another reason to keep fighting for my health. I've got a grandbaby I'll need to be spry enough to chase after soon."

For the sake of my child, I hoped I had her strength. "I should probably shower and chase down Cooper before he disappears again. I need to ask him to be tested for the Festner's gene. There's an in-utero treatment for it now, but it's time sensitive."

Her hand came to her mouth. "You have no idea how relieved I am to hear that there's a treatment now."

"Which hopefully won't even be necessary. He might not have the gene." I swallowed hard. "I hope he agrees to the testing."

"He will." She gave my hand a squeeze then stood. "When your father asked me if it was okay for Cooper to move in above the store I was afraid he might be a problem. Instead he's been a blessing."

I swung my feet out from under the blankets and lowered them to the floor. "How are you not shocked by any of this?"

At the door of my bedroom she turned and met my gaze. "Amanda, the two of you are meant to be together. The whole town knows it."

"The whole town, well, then who am I to question that?" Shaking my head, I stood. "Mom, he left without saying a word. It's been weeks and I haven't heard from him."

Her eyebrows rose at the bite in my tone. "Maybe if you'd dated him a time or two before . . ."

My mouth rounded and I held back all the snarky things I could have responded with because she was my mother and as usual she was . . . right.

"Just a thought." She softened her comment with a wink then closed the door behind her.

Dating Cooper had never been an option, but not by my choice. I thought back to when I was seventeen and had dated Wyatt Spavold in what was in hindsight clearly an attempt to make Cooper jealous. It hadn't worked. I'd ended up getting my pride hurt when it turned out Wyatt moved on to date someone who actually liked him.

I shook my head at the memory of how immature and self-absorbed I'd been. Whatever might have been possible between Wyatt and me had been yet another casualty of my mini-obsession with Cooper.

I'd been angry with myself, with Wyatt, and even Cooper until I'd come home from school the next day to find Cooper had planted a garden of my favorite flowers right next to my outdoor reading spot. He had a way of making me feel special and cared about without ever letting me into his life.

I kept waiting for him to let me in, and there'd been hints that he might. The week after Aunt Roselyn died

Cooper had come to sit with me on the back porch every evening. When my childhood dog, Patches, had to be put down, he'd helped me bury her near the tree she used to nap under. Even when I'd left for college, Cooper had been right there, helping me pack my car and checking that my tires had air.

Always there—and not at the same time. It was enough to keep my heart in painful limbo. It wasn't that I couldn't find men willing to take me out, but none of them touched my heart. None looked at me the way Cooper did or suspended time the way he did every time he was near.

After showering and dressing, I gathered my phone but hesitated before leaving my room. No matter how Cooper and I did or didn't feel about one another, the life we'd created was depending on us now. That was what was important . . . not if my pride was hurt or if the conversation I needed to have with Cooper was going to be uncomfortable.

With or without him, my baby would be taken care of. All I needed from him was a blood test. I couldn't see why he'd have a problem with that.

Everything is going to work out.

Chapter Ten

Cooper

I HAD JUST stepped out of the backdoor of the hardware store and was walking toward my truck when I heard Amanda call out my name. I froze, then slowly turned on my heel to greet her. She rushed to me, flushed and breathless. My body came to life beneath her gaze. Damn, she was even more beautiful. How was that possible? "Morning."

"Cooper, we need to talk."

I fought back X-rated memories from the last time we'd attempted that. *This is not about that. Well, probably related, but not in a good way.*

And that was a mistake I don't intend to make again.

She was visibly upset. She had every right to be. I had no defense for my behavior, at least none I was willing to offer. "Of course. Do you want to get a coffee?"

"No. This is a conversation we should have alone."

There was an urgency to her I wasn't sure how to interpret. She didn't appear angry as I'd first thought. She couldn't be hoping for a repeat of the last time. Could she? Fuck. That thought was all it took for my cock to decide to be ready just in case. "It's probably better if we don't—"

"No. That's not—" Her eyes widened then narrowed and I waited. Eventually her hands went to her hips and she cocked her head to one side. "That's not why I'm here."

"Oh, good." I didn't mean to say that aloud. And it didn't reflect how I really felt. I would have loved nothing more than to sweep her up into my arms and carry her off to the nearest private spot. My relief stemmed from knowing that I wouldn't be strong enough to deny her if that was what she wanted too. For this to work, for me to keep my hands off her, she needed to not want to be with me. That was proving easier than anticipated. If looks could kill I would have been dead, dead, dead. "I didn't mean to say that as bluntly as I did."

She raised a finger between us, took a deep breath, lowered her finger then raised it again. "I'm not doing this. I'm not getting into some silly fight with you just because we had sex and now things are weird. We're both adults. We can put our feelings aside and have a civil conversation." She clasped her hands in front of her. "At least I hope we can."

My body clenched and I bent closer. "Has something happened?"

She looked away before meeting my gaze again. "You could say that."

On full alert now, nothing mattered more than making sure she was okay. I took hold of one of her arms. "What? Is it your parents? You? What do you need?"

She glanced around and made a face. "I didn't really want to have this conversation in an alley, but whatever. I'm pregnant, Cooper."

"Pregnant?" My hand must have tightened on her arm because she pulled it free and frowned.

"Three weeks."

"Three weeks?" It took a moment for that to sink in. "It's mine?"

Her glare said it all.

She's pregnant.

The weight of it crushed in. I thought of all the times I'd been hyper-careful because I couldn't live with the idea of cursing a child to a life with a father who could never really be there for him. There was a reason I didn't use my real social security number—everything about me was a lie. "You're certain?"

She blinked quickly then sniffed and placed a hand protectively over her stomach. "Yes, and before you ask, I'm having it."

"I would never suggest—" I stopped there. Had she opted to not have it I would have supported that choice as well. Honestly I was still trying to wrap my head around that she was pregnant. "I'm sorry."

I was . . . sorry that I hadn't used a condom . . . that I wasn't in the position to step up and be the kind of father a child should have. I was infinitely sorry I'd repaid Pete's kindness to me by knocking up his daughter.

Her stance relaxed. "Me too. I was just as shocked when I got the news. It took me a little bit to adjust to the idea, but I'm trying to see it as an unexpected blessing."

I nodded, even though that was far from how I saw it. I

ran a hand through my hair and let out a long breath. *I just keep fucking up.*

Leaving would be complicated now, but I could send money from anywhere. Tom would funnel finances to Amanda for me. I'd make sure no one could make a connection between me and the baby—for the baby's safety. "Financially, I'll do whatever you and the baby need." I'd been generous with my money in the past so I didn't have much saved, but I wasn't afraid of hard work.

"*Financially*, the baby and I will be fine." She looked so sad and I'd never hated myself more than I did in that moment. "What we need from you is—"

"Money is all I have to give," I said, cutting her off.

Her expression tightened. "Wow. You don't even know what I'm going to say and you already know you can't do it? What is it about me that you hate? I've seen you help the Johnsons clean out their basement because their septic system backed up. That was literally a shitty job and you did it with no complaints. I need to ask you for one thing . . . for the child you helped bring into this world . . . and you already know you can't do it? Whatever problem you have with me, let's figure it out now, because whether you want to be or not you're the father of this child. Don't punish it because you and I can't figure each other out."

That gutted me.

"There is nothing I hate about you." I brought a hand up to rub over my eyes. "You've never been the problem. Never."

She touched my arm. "Then listen. There's something I

need to talk to you about. Have you ever heard of Festner's disease?"

"No." I lowered my hand as what she'd asked sunk in. Was she ill? It couldn't somehow be related to her mother's cancer, could it? All kinds of crazy thoughts went through my head. "What is it?"

"It's a condition that causes a high mortality rate in infants. It runs in my family."

Worse than her being pregnant was the idea that she might lose the baby. I swayed on my feet. "You think the baby has it?"

"It may. I carry the recessive gene for the disease. If you do as well, my doctor suggested we start treatment right away. The gene therapy is most successful in the first trimester."

"I don't believe it runs in my family."

"The only way to know for sure is to do genetic testing on a blood sample. My doctor gave me paperwork for you. She was hoping you could drive to the lab today. That's all I need. I can have the results in days then schedule the treatment if necessary." She searched my face. "Will you do it?"

"Give blood," I said slowly. With all the advancements made in technology having a DNA test might instantly expose me. It didn't help that my false ID might not pass that level of inspection. "I don't have health insurance; will that be a problem?"

Her mouth rounded. "You don't have health insurance?"

It was difficult to get with a fake social security number. "Never needed it."

"That's no good, Cooper. What would you do if you got really sick?"

I shrugged. I didn't allow myself to think about that. Staying out of databases was how I'd remained invisible. I didn't want to open that door, but the baby's life over mine was an easy choice. Still, it was worth asking, "Would they allow an anonymous blood sample? I don't want to be billed." The last part was the first excuse I could think of for why I didn't want my name linked to the baby's. The possibility that someone might one day come for me had always been in the back of my mind, and was another reason I hadn't let anyone too close.

I should have left.

I should have been strong enough to send her home.

Disgust filled her eyes. "If you're charged for the testing, I'll make sure the bill is paid."

I hated what she thought of me, but there wasn't much I could say without telling her everything. I'd decided a long time ago that the less people knew the safer they'd be. If the law came for me, I didn't want anyone implicated in covering up my crimes. If my relatives came, I needed to be their only target.

Anger turned to sadness in her eyes. "I can't claim to understand you, Cooper. On one hand you've been so good to me and my family. On the other hand, at least when it comes to me, you can be so cold." She hugged her arms around her waist. "I want you to be part of the baby's life, but I don't know if the way we are with each other would be healthy for them to see."

Between gritted teeth, I said, "The baby doesn't need to know me."

"How can you say that?" She inhaled sharply and straightened to her full height. "All it requires is for us to be friends." Tears welled in her eyes. "Is that really such an impossible request?"

It shouldn't have been. She was right, though, regardless of what I was comfortable with or thought would be best, this was happening. I wasn't a praying man, but I prayed then.

Don't do this.

They're innocent.

I'd sworn I would never take another life, but as I looked down into Amanda's eyes I felt capable of killing anyone who would hurt her or our baby. Was it time to stand and fight instead of hide? Could I keep them safe if I did? I was one man—a nearly broke one at that. There was only one person who would benefit from me disappearing for good, my brother Clay. He'd have the resources to send in an army of hitmen and pay off officials at all levels to look the other way.

Would he do that? After all the time that had passed? I wanted to think he wouldn't, but money brought out the evil in people. I'd seen it firsthand. My family was ripe with tragedies wrought by greed. So, yes, if Clay discovered I was alive and he felt I threatened any portion of his inheritance he'd erase the problem.

When it came to protecting their fortunes, there was no low my relatives wouldn't sink to. My gaze fell to Amanda's flat stomach. If I was a threat . . . our baby would be seen as one as well. My hands fisted at my sides.

I won't let that happen.

"Can they test the baby for the gene without testing me?" Even as I asked the question I hated myself for voicing it. That would only buy us time. Testing the baby would put its DNA into data bases as well. Eventually someone would make the connection.

I needed a plan.

Amanda made a frustrated sound that confused me then threw her hands up in the air. "I can't believe you!" Blood started pouring out of one of her nostrils. She brought a hand to dab at the stream pooling above her lip. "Fuck."

I stepped closer. "Are you okay?" I didn't know if she was about to pass out so I hovered my hands around her, ready for anything.

She dug a wad of tissues out of her pocket and held it to her nose. "No, I'm not. None of this is okay. I can't believe I'm getting a bloody nose right now. Just go . . . before I decide to get that blood sample by punching you in the nose."

"Tip your head forward and pinch just below the bone."

She leaned forward and did as I suggested. "I know how to handle it. I've been getting these a lot."

"Is that normal?" It didn't sound normal. "Does your doctor know?"

"Please don't pretend to be concerned."

I hovered close. "It may not seem like it, Amanda, but I do care about you." There was a high probability I'd love her straight until my last breath. "And the baby."

She didn't look convinced. "We're both fine. My mother used to get nosebleeds when she was pregnant with me." I couldn't blame her for doubting me.

My hand stilled. "So your parents know."

"My mother does. She hasn't told my father yet and I haven't worked up the courage to yet."

"I'll tell him."

Her eyes flew to mine. "I'm sure that would go over well."

I shrugged. My relationship with Pete came second to making sure Amanda had the support she needed. With all that Dotty had been through recently, I hated that I'd added to her stress. "How did your mother take it?"

Amanda dabbed at an area below her nose then straightened her neck. "That wasn't so bad."

"Telling your mother?"

"No, the nosebleed. I've had much worse. I didn't have to tell my mother, she guessed. And she's thrilled about the idea of a grandchild."

Thank God for that. I cleared my throat. "Your father will be happy too." *After he strangles me.*

"And you?"

I took one of the still clean tissues from her hand and wiped away a few spots of blood on her face she'd missed. In that moment I felt connected to her in a way that went beyond sexual attraction. I wanted to care for her and the baby, to be part of it all—the good, the bad, the bloody. I wanted it so badly I almost couldn't breathe. Her eyes were huge and so trusting. She and the baby needed me. I'd find a way to deal with my relatives. "I'll give a blood sample."

And then I'll get a security system for the Glenford household.

A gun.

Possibly a lawyer.

"Thank you." She almost wiped at the corner of her eye with the bloody tissue, then made a face. After glancing around she tossed her tissues in a trash dumpster.

I did the same with the ones I'd taken from her. "There are perks to hanging out in an alley."

She didn't smile, but I hadn't given her much reason to.

"Oh, good, you're still here," Levi said from behind me. "Hope I'm not interrupting anything."

Although it was hard, I pulled my attention from Amanda to greet him. "Perfect timing as always." Levi had once thrown a surprise party for Mr. Tissbury the same day he had a pacemaker put in. Thankfully no one died that day, but we'd never let Levi live it down.

"Hey, Amanda," Levi said in the casual tone of someone who'd known her his whole life, because he had.

"Hi, Levi." Amanda greeted him with a warm smile.

"I thought you weren't coming back until the weekend."

She shrugged. "Changed my mind. It's really not that bad of a drive."

His smile widened and he motioned toward me. "Not when you've got a reason to make it."

"Stop, Levi," I said more harshly than I meant to. I didn't like that he might know Amanda and I had hooked up, but it shouldn't have surprised me if the whole town did. Nothing went unnoticed in Driverton.

Levi raised both hands in mock surrender. "Sorry. Right. I know nothing."

I sighed. "Did you need something?"

Levi shrugged. "Ollie told me you were back in town. Had to come see what condition you're in. Sometimes it ain't all that good."

Amanda frowned in confusion and I motioned for Levi to drop the subject. "Everything went smoothly this time, just took a little longer than I'd anticipated."

Levi looked from me to Amanda and back. "We can talk about it later."

"Or not at all," I countered.

He winked. "Right. I'll see you at Little Willie's later."

"Not today." With everything else going on, it wasn't the time to tell Amanda about where I'd been. She probably had some idea. It would have been impossible to hide something like my extended disappearances from everyone in town, especially when there'd been times when I'd returned in need of medical assistance.

Like my life before Driverton, what Tom and I did was kept on the downlow. Tom risked his retirement every time he involved me in a case. We lied, bribed, threatened . . . when it came to locating those kids, we did what we needed to.

Levi knew more than most because he and Tom's sister, Katie, were tight. Levi told me she talked to him about it because she was proud of her brother. That pride might one day land Tom in legal trouble. Katie was sweet, but could she keep her mouth shut if an investigation ever happened? For Tom's sake, I hoped so.

"That's a shame," Levi said. "My mother made meat loaf today. I could have brought you a slice."

Tempting. His mother was an amazing cook. "I love her meat loaf, but I do need to get some errands done."

He wiggled his eyebrows. "Sure. Errands. Whatever you want to call it."

The look I gave him wiped the smile off his face. He turned to Amanda and said, "Sorry. I'm really happy for the two of you. Everyone is."

"Thanks, Levi," Amanda said in a choked voice.

He thumbed toward the street. "I guess I'll see you both around."

I nodded once.

Amanda's smile looked forced.

Before walking away, Levi said, "Hey, Amanda. Mel and Mike are having a bonfire tomorrow night. You should come. We were all saying how great it is to have you back."

Amanda's smile transformed. "It's good to be back. Tell Mel I'll be there."

She belongs in this town.

I need to make sure she's safe here.

"Cooper?"

I met her gaze again. "Yes?"

"Do you want to be there when I tell my father about the baby?"

"Yes." Pete needed to know so he could help keep her

safe.

"Now?" Amanda asked. "Or after you go to Bangor for the blood test?"

My admiration for Amanda and her grit grew as she stood there, looking me in the eye. None of the conversation we'd had could have been easy for her, but she hadn't backed down. She was going to be one hell of a mother.

"Now." The enormity of Amanda being pregnant was hitting me in waves. "I'm going to be a father."

She pressed her lips together briefly, then said, "It's scary, isn't it?"

"You have no idea."

"I might have a hint." She rolled her eyes at me then started walking away. "I'll meet you at my parents' house."

Chapter Eleven

Amanda

I SHOULD HAVE made Cooper come with me.

What if he leaves again?

What if he doesn't go to the lab?

My hands were tight on my steering wheel as I drove to my parents' house. Nothing made sense. The Cooper I knew wasn't unreliable. He was the person people knew they could call day or night when they were in need.

I hadn't expected him to be overjoyed to hear we'd accidentally created a life, but his response was so disappointing I was still reeling from it. After parking in my parents' driveway, I took a moment to gather my thoughts.

None of it made sense.

Where did Cooper go? Why did he come back from there in bad shape? Why did everyone seem to know about it and not want to talk about it?

My father had said Cooper might be too broken for any of us to fix. Why? How? What did everyone but me know?

There was a time when respecting Cooper's need for privacy was more important than my curiosity. I'd followed my parents' philosophy of letting people share more of themselves on their own terms. I wasn't ready to do that anymore.

Because it's not just about me this time.

The baby needs Cooper to get that blood test.

Part of me had known it would be an issue, and that made even less sense to me. How could I feel anything for a man I was sure would disappoint me? Being near him shouldn't have felt as good as it did. I should be angry with him, but instead all I felt was deep sadness and disappointment.

Along with the oddest urge to hug him and tell him everything was going to be okay. Him? Why would I feel he needed comforting? *I'm the one having a baby.*

I'm the one whose entire life is currently upside down.

What is wrong with me?

I looked out over the grass field behind my parents' house and remembered the day I'd spontaneously decided I might be an equestrian. Mrs. Tissbury asked if someone could ride her old mare to help keep her in shape. I'd ridden a horse once or twice before and thought it would be easy. I learned that day that mares can dole out hefty lessons in humility.

What started as a quiet ride through my parents' back field turned into a wild race with the wind followed by some rodeo-style bucking that sent me sailing through the air. I'd landed in a way that not only knocked the wind out of me but also twisted my ankle badly. Cooper had appeared as he always had when I was in need. He'd checked that nothing was broken then carried me to my house. Without being asked to, he'd collected the mare, returned her to Mrs. Tissbury, then returned with ice and a wrap for my ankle.

Always there. Always my guardian angel.

How could that Cooper not want to be part of his child's life? I wanted to shake him until that made sense to me. Had he only taken care of me out of a sense of gratitude for what my parents had done for him? Was there something he found repulsive about me? Not so repulsive he couldn't sleep with me . . . just enough that he didn't want me in his life.

Cooper's truck pulled up behind my car and I inhaled deeply a few times, telling myself that none of the emotions rampaging within me would help the situation. For the sake of my parents, this needed to be done calmly. My mother was doing better, getting stronger every day. I would not be the reason she had a setback.

My father wasn't going to be happy at first, but only because he worried. Once he saw I was okay, he would be too.

I needed to warn Cooper if he showed my father the side of himself he'd just shown me, he'd lose my father's respect. I didn't want that to happen. I let myself out of my car and slammed the door behind me.

Cooper came to stand in front of me, looking more miserable than any man who'd just learned he was going to be a father should. I wanted to kick him in the shin and then hug him or the reverse. "Let me tell him," I said in a tight voice. "My father adores you. We might be able to do this in a way that doesn't destroy that."

He held my gaze without responding but walked with me when I turned to make my way to the steps of my parents' porch. My father opened the door. He looked from me to Cooper and back.

I stopped near my father and searched his face. My father was usually an easy read, but not this time. Did he know? I couldn't tell. "Cooper and I have something we need to talk to you and Mom about."

My father made a sound deep in his throat. "Do you?" His attention stayed on Cooper.

Cooper inhaled audibly and held my father's gaze. "And a few things we should discuss on the side."

They exchanged a look I didn't understand or like. Just what did they think needed to be said that I couldn't hear? I opened my mouth to say as much but my mother appeared behind my father and said, "Come on in, you two. Is anyone hungry?"

"No," the three of us answered in unison.

"There's always room for a little something." She took me by the hand. "I just made fresh muffins. Why don't you help me put some on a plate?"

I resisted the slight tug she gave me. "After we talk, Mom." It wasn't like she didn't know what we'd come to say.

With a nod and hand squeeze of support, she said, "Okay, but let's at least come into the house. No need to stay out on the porch like we're strangers."

I let her lead me into the living room where she and I took a seat on one of the couches. She still tired quickly and this wasn't going to be an easy conversation.

Cooper and my father followed us into the living room

but remained standing, facing each other, both looking as tense as I felt. I spoke first. "Dad, I'm pregnant. Cooper is the father. I need you to be okay with this."

For several heartbeats no one moved or said a word.

In a soft tone, my mother said, "Your father knows, Amanda. We talked about it after you left. Pete, say something."

Still, my father remained silent as did Cooper. They stood there looking at each other in what I could only guess was some male form of communication.

Cooper cleared his throat. "I'm sorry, Pete."

My father straightened to his full height. "You think that's what I'm waiting to hear you say?"

Cooper's face tightened and he blinked a few times. "If I could say anything else I would."

That he loved me?

That he'd be there for me?

What couldn't he say?

I rose to my feet and stood between the two men. Those questions could wait. They had to. "Dad, Cooper agreed to have genetic testing done. I just thought you should know where he's going today."

"Agreed to?" My father gave me a quick look then returned his attention to Cooper. "Sounds like it wasn't an automatic yes." His eyes narrowed. "It should have been."

I looked to my mother for help. I wasn't handling this as well as I'd hoped. She went to stand beside my father and slipped beneath his arm to hug him. "Amanda doesn't need you to protect her from Cooper, she needs your support."

My father's eyes flew to mine. "She knows she has that." He looked at Cooper again. "Just like Cooper knows where my loyalty lies."

Cooper said in a quiet tone, "Which is why we should talk after this—alone."

There it was . . . another reference to the missing piece of the puzzle. I touched Cooper's arm. "Anything you feel you need to say to my father, you should say to me. I'm the one carrying the baby."

His eyes darkened and the muscles in his arm tightened. He seemed conflicted, but then sighed and said, "My name isn't Cooper Davis. I'm 26, not 28. I use a fake social security number and a fake license. Everything you think you know about me is probably wrong and there's a good chance that once I give the lab a DNA sample I'll need to leave town again—for good."

"Why would you need to leave?" I asked just above a whisper. The rest was something I'd put out of my thoughts, but that a part of me had always known. Hearing it, though, wasn't clarifying anything for me.

Cooper's expression was tortured. "My priority is your safety." He glanced around at my parents. "All of you."

My father demanded, "Is this because of what you do with Sheriff Tom?"

Cooper shook his head. "No. That's a secret to protect him, not me."

"Secret?" I gave Cooper's arm a shake. "What are you talking about? What do you and Tom do?"

My father answered before Cooper had a chance to.

"They locate runaways and kidnapped children and rescue them."

My grip tightened on Cooper's forearm as I searched his face. "You do that?"

There was no pride in his eyes, just more sadness. "Someone has to and being invisible has its advantages."

My hand dropped from Cooper's arm. I fought to stay calm but how could I have become so out of touch with my own hometown? "I had no idea."

This time Cooper reached out to me, but stopped before actually touching me. "There was no need for you to."

"No need?" My voice thickened. I glanced around at my parents. "I didn't move away because I didn't care about what happens here."

My mother left my father to put an arm around me. "We know that, hon. There was just never the right time to bring it up. You and Cooper weren't . . ."

We still weren't.

Cooper and Tom were saving runaway children? That fit everything I knew about both of them. Both were good men who were not afraid to step up to help those in need. Still, it begged another question. I turned to face Cooper. "If you care about other children, why wouldn't you care about your own?"

Cooper stepped back as if I'd hit him. "I do, but I don't know the best way to handle this. I need time to—"

"What you need is to fucking be honest with me." My nerves were frayed, and I couldn't hold back.

My mother said, "Amanda—"

"She has the right to demand answers," my father cut in. "Cooper, we gave you a fresh place to start over. We respected that you didn't want to talk about where you came from or what happened to you. Our home has always been open to you, but how you deal with this—who you prove yourself to be right here and now, that will determine how welcome you'll be from here on."

Cooper looked from my father to me again. "You do deserve the truth." He let out a breath. "I never wanted to put any of you in danger."

I swallowed hard. "Why would we be in danger, Cooper? Talk to us."

He looked down, then away. "Once you know, you'll understand why I should have stayed away from you, Amanda. I should have stayed away from all of you."

That sent a chill down my back, but I could never be afraid of Cooper. He and I had once seen a stray cat trying to retrieve her kittens from under a pile of wooden pallets during a thunderstorm and gotten soaked as we'd saved them together. That cat and those kittens had stayed in his apartment until we'd found homes for all of them. No, I couldn't fear him, but I was afraid of whatever had him worried for our safety.

If it scared Cooper . . .

My father's stance remained rigid. "Say what you need to say, son. It's time."

Cooper nodded. "I was born into an extremely wealthy family." He raised a hand as if pleading for us to hold off on saying anything about that. "Which might sound like a privilege, but it's been nothing but a curse. With wealth comes power and greed. My reappearance could be seen as a threat to some who would assume I'm interested in my inheritance. In my experience, that's enough to get a person eliminated."

"Eliminated?" my mother asked in a high voice. "Like killed?"

I turned to better support her. "I'm sure that's not what he—"

Cooper continued, "I've been gone ten years so I can't say for certain what will happen when it becomes known that I'm still alive, but I know what my family is capable of." He straightened his shoulders. "I won't be returning to Driverton after I do the blood test. I can't sit back and wait to see what my family will do. I need to do something."

"Not alone." The words were wrung out of me. He was one of us. We protected each other.

A fire lit his eyes. "That's the way it has to be, Amanda. You can't know the details or be a part of anything I do. The only reason I'm telling you this is because you need to be careful, all of you. Don't trust anyone you don't know. For now, the fewer who know about the baby, the better. I don't intend to fail, but if I do, those who would come for me would come for my child."

My hands flew up to protect my stomach. "No."

"Money brings out the ugliest side of people," Cooper said in a cold voice. "Even me. I thought I was free of it, but it looks like I need to go another round with this demon."

"Cooper, you're not alone. We'll figure this out together."

Cooper laughed without humor. "You don't know who we're dealing with." He turned to address my father. "I hate that this is how I'm repaying all you've done for me, but I promise I will do everything in my power to make sure my curse doesn't visit this town."

"Who *are* you?" my father demanded. "What's your real last name?"

"Cooper Landon."

"As in the Landon Foundation?" my mother asked.

"If it's run by Clay Landon, then yes."

My mother added, "That is who runs it, I believe." She looked to my father. "With the Gold Star Program for families of fallen soldiers. That's the one your friends talk about, isn't it?"

Even I'd heard about that program. "Clay Landon is said to be one of the wealthiest people in the world." My parents nodded. I asked Cooper, "He's related to you?"

"He's my brother."

I let that one sink in. "I read an article about him once. He came into money when his grandparents died. There was no mention of siblings."

"It's just Clay and me now," Cooper said.

"There were others?" my father asked.

"Yes. Both were older. A brother and a sister."

"Were?" My mother looked as shaken as I was by this conversation.

"Both dead, along with my parents. I believed one was an accident and the other an overdose, but then I was told I would be 'dealt with' the same way they were. So your guess is as good as mine when it comes to how they actually died."

I swayed on my feet and the room began to spin. "I should sit down."

Cooper's arm was instantly around my waist. He walked me back to the couch, then sat beside me. "You don't need to know all this or even believe it. All you need to do is take care of yourself and this baby. I'll handle the rest."

"Amanda's right. You shouldn't go through this alone," my mother said firmly. "Pete, call Tom. He needs to hear this. After everything Cooper has done for him, with him, Tom will want to help."

"He won't," Cooper protested.

"Don't underestimate his loyalty to you," my father said as he took out his phone and started texting. "He could arrange for police protection while you sort this out."

"You don't understand." Cooper ran a hand through his hair. "Tom won't be able to help me and if I end up in jail I can't stop my family."

"He's on his way," my father said. "Tom isn't going to turn you in for having a false ID. I'm sure he already knows. Hell, we all guessed Davis wasn't your last name."

Cooper nodded, but looked on the verge of getting phys-ically sick. I took one of his hands in mine. "Whatever you're afraid of, whatever you think is coming for you . . . look around. You're not alone this time. You know how much you're willing to do to keep me safe? That's how we feel about helping you. I know it's not easy, but you can trust us."

His hand tightened on mine. "If you knew everything you'd understand why you can't be involved."

I couldn't imagine anything he'd say that could change the way I felt about him, but that didn't make it any easier to wait for Tom to arrive. I let out a shaky breath, rose to my feet, and said, "I need something to settle my stomach. Cooper, could you come to the kitchen with me for a minute?"

"Of course," Cooper said from my side a heartbeat later.

My father didn't look happy about us stepping away, but my mother spoke to him softly and seemed to convince him to let us go. I didn't say anything until Cooper and I were in the kitchen, out of earshot of my parents. Leaning back against a counter and gripping it on either side of me, I burst out, "Holy shit, Cooper. What else have you not told us?"

Chapter Twelve

Cooper

"DO YOU TRUST me, Amanda?"

Her pause before answering was as telling as her response. "I'm trying to."

"Then don't ask questions you're better off not knowing the answers to. I don't put a lot of stock in my life, but I care about the people in Driverton."

"Don't say that," she said in an emotional rush.

"That I care?" I asked even though I knew what she'd been referring to.

"God, you are so . . . so aggravating. There's something you don't want us to know—I get it. You want to forget it ever happened. I understand that too. But stop lying to yourself about why you've never talked about it. You say it's about protecting us, but I'm beginning to believe it's about protecting yourself. What do you think will happen if you tell us?"

Her question rocked through me. I didn't look back at my life before Driverton because I hated who I was back then. I needed to believe that wasn't who I still was.

My silence did protect me, but I'd held to it because I never wanted Amanda or anyone in town to be drawn into the legal mess stalking me.

Over the years I'd read enough case law to understand that once I shared the details of what I'd done, anyone who knew and helped me avoid detection from the law could be considered accessories to murder after the fact.

Should I simply tell her that?

I had a strong feeling that answer would only lead to more questions. What I needed was time to figure out how to shield Amanda and the others without implicating them.

The silence in the kitchen was heavy and prolonged. Eventually she lowered her hands to her sides. "You're not going to tell me, are you?"

I wanted to, but I didn't give myself that comfort. My uncle had always said that Clay had chosen to go with our grandparents because he wanted to take control of their fortune. His plan had apparently worked. Clay had inherited everything. I had no real memories of my eldest brother beyond the arguments he had with Caterina and the stories from our uncle about how cunning and ruthless he was.

What would someone like Clay do when he learned I was still alive? The only way to know would be to get closer to him and watch for a pattern of behavior. I couldn't formulate a plan of action on how to deal with the threat of him until I evaluated the threat itself.

How far would I go to protect Amanda and the others?

As far as I had to.

"Tom is here," Pete called from the door of the kitchen.

Amanda pushed off from the counter. She was shaking her head with a disappointed expression I was once again responsible for. "Perfect timing. We're done in here anyway."

I stepped in front of her. "Amanda, I—"

"Don't." She waved a hand at me. "It's fine. I'm the one who keeps pushing my way into your life. All I want from you now is the blood sample. I'm done trying to figure you out."

I moved aside to let her pass. She'd left the kitchen, but Pete remained at the door even as I approached it. "Amanda has very good instincts when it comes to reading people."

"She was right this time as well." I stopped a few feet from the door, half expecting him to tell me to leave through the other door and never return. "I've done worse than create a fake ID. If I tell Tom the truth, he'll be forced to make a choice between the oath he took and me. I can't put him in that position."

Pete crossed his arms over his chest. "You're talking to someone who knows you, Cooper. Whatever you did, I'm sure you had a reason to."

"You don't know that." Not even I was sure both had been as necessary as they'd felt in the moment.

"Tom's waiting for us." Pete nodded toward the living room. "Tell him everything or tell him nothing. From what you've already shared, I understand why you might not have much faith in family, but to me it's everything. Trust goes both ways, son. You want us on your side, you'll have to tell us what you're running from."

"I'm not running from anything, not anymore."

Pete took a moment to weigh that, then said, "You're the father of my grandchild. To us, that means you're family now. Are you? That's up to you."

Without waiting for me to respond, he turned and walked away. The Glenfords weren't perfect, but when things got tough, they pulled together rather than apart as my family had. I stood, temporarily frozen as I debated what I should do next.

Would I ever get it right with Amanda? All I'd ever wanted to do was protect her. All I seemed to be doing was hurting her. Her expression as she'd left the kitchen stayed with me as did her words. She'd never pushed her way into my life. What she'd done was give me chance after chance to be part of hers . . . more than I deserved.

Pete was the same. He could have thrown me out of his house. I wouldn't have blamed him if he'd warned me to stay away from Amanda. Instead he'd given me another chance to be part of his family.

What was the right thing to do? Let them in and possibly put them all at risk? Keep them at a distance and hurt them in an entirely different way?

Dotty appeared at the kitchen door. "Cooper?"

"Sorry." I kept my eyes averted. "I need a minute."

She stepped into the room and stopped in front of me. "Are you okay?"

"Not really." In a burst of honesty, I said, "I don't know what to do, Dotty. There's no good option."

"I didn't come in here because I have any answers for

you. I just wanted to tell you that I love you. We all do." A little humor entered her voice as she added, "Not all of us are happy with you right now, but that happens."

"Yeah." That they cared about me had never been in question.

Her expression turned more serious. "What you said about your family earlier . . . Do you know how strong you are to have survived that?"

I shook my head. "I don't feel strong. Most of the time, if I feel anything at all, it's anger."

She placed a hand on one of my shoulders. "I know that feeling well."

That shocked me and my eyes flew to hers.

She continued, "Cancer sucks. Every part of it."

I nodded in support and was humbled. There I was hating my life while Dotty was fighting for hers. "But you've beaten it."

She gave me a long look. "That's what the doctors say. I can't shake the feeling, though, that my body betrayed me once so it will again. And that makes me angry."

"I imagine it would." I didn't know what else to say.

"Anger is a curious thing. You have to choose it for it to have any power. Whenever I wake up and I feel more tired than when I went to bed, anger visits me. But now I look it in the eye and I say—I don't choose you today. Then I seek out things that make me happy: a sunrise, my husband's smile, a walk with Amanda, and I choose gratitude for those things. Gratitude is the bread that makes a happiness sandwich possible. Without it, all you have is a pile of sliced turkey, lettuce, and mayo with a layer or two of cheese." She paused, lowered her hand, and smiled. "Sorry, I guess I'm hungry. It was a better analogy until I started imagining it and salivating."

I chuckled. "That's okay, I get the idea." In a more serious tone I added, "I do have a lot I'm grateful for."

"Then choose that." She linked an arm with mine and gave me a tug toward the living room. "And us. You might not know what to do, but there are three people in the other room who want to help you figure that out. Let them."

I blinked a few times quickly. "Dotty . . ." The words were on the tip of my tongue, but impossible to voice.

She hugged my arm as we walked. "I love you too, Cooper."

Chapter Thirteen

Amanda

WHEN MY MOTHER had said she'd retrieve Cooper from the kitchen I'd still been irritated enough with him that I hadn't cared if she was successful. Tom and my father had moved to the side of the room to talk. It bothered me, but not enough to interrupt them.

Once I'd had a few minutes to cool down, I admitted to myself that I wasn't angry with Cooper, I was embarrassed. For a minute there I'd really thought he would open up to me. Me before anyone else. Why? Because in my heart I felt I was special to him.

To get to a healthy place where Cooper and I could talk without fighting, I needed to let that fantasy go. We'd had sex. We were having a baby. We needed to at least be amicable.

My mother returned from the kitchen with a much calmer looking Cooper. He surprised me by coming to stand beside me instead of joining Tom and my father as my mother did. When he bent his head so he could say something only I'd hear, I tensed and prayed a little. Was he about to tell me he was really leaving for good? I wasn't ready for that.

"I'm sorry I make you feel that you care about me more than I care about you. It's not true."

When our eyes met the air sizzled with emotion as well as desire. Fresh from feeling stupid about reading more into our connection than there was, I fought to take his apology on face value. Of course he cared about me—we'd been part of each other's lives for over a decade. Considering the close relationship he had with my parents, it would have been odd if he didn't care about me. Caring was very different than craving. Nothing had changed except that he'd once again removed my ability to be upset with him. "Thank you. I'm sorry about what I said in the kitchen. I was embarrassed—"

He bent closer, his breath a tickle on my ear as he said, "Never be embarrassed with me."

I nodded and inhaled sharply. God, it was so easy with Cooper. All he had to do was stand beside me and my body longed for more. I met his gaze again, flushed from head to toe, then forced myself to look away.

Tom crossed the room to join us. "Cooper *Landon*."

My father had apparently brought Tom up to speed. At my side, Cooper straightened. "That's the name I was born with," Cooper said.

"Landons." Tom rubbed a hand over the back of his neck. "I don't know a lot about them, but it looks like that's about to change."

"This isn't a job you should associate yourself with, Tom. If it goes bad, it's going to go really bad. You'd be better off with no search record that would hint at your involvement. Someone has to stay here and keep everyone safe."

I shuddered beside Cooper. His tone was cold and clipped. Where was the Cooper from a moment before? I swallowed hard then asked, "Cooper, what kind of job are you considering?"

Tom answered before him, "Nothing he'll do until I understand the situation better."

"You couldn't stop me if you tried," Cooper said firmly.

Tom's head snapped back and he looked a little offended. "If the shit Pete was telling me is true, there's no risk I'd try to stop you—but I will help you. This isn't a battle you can win alone."

My parents joined us, but my attention stayed riveted to Cooper. "You really believe your brother will send someone to hurt us?"

Cooper's shoulders rose and fell before he answered. "I'm not willing to sit back and wait to find out."

"There are legal options, Cooper," Tom said. "Pete suggested someone be assigned to watch over you and Amanda. I can't get that without proof of need, but I'm in. I'll gather whatever evidence we need to make that happen."

Shaking his head, Cooper said, "If you start looking for evidence, I'm sure you'll find some, but it won't just be against them. I haven't only been hiding from my family. There's a good chance that when my DNA hits a database you'll see my face pop up, attached to an arrest warrant."

Thinking about the condition he'd originally arrived in, I

said, "For robbing someplace? You were a minor and enough time has passed I'm sure it has exceeded that statute of limitation for something like that." I didn't condone stealing, but a kid on the run didn't have many options. He and Tom were saving missing children, Cooper had more than repaid that debt.

After taking a deep breath, Cooper said, "There is no statute of limitation on murder and I took two lives."

My mother's hands came to her chest. My father put an arm around her but held his silence. I shook my head in disbelief. "You wouldn't do that."

Cooper held my gaze, his eyes dark with emotion. "I did. I can tell myself they deserved to die. I can spend the rest of my life trying to make up for what I did, but the truth is that I crossed that line—twice."

Tom looked as skeptical as I felt. "When? How? Was it an accident?"

In a cold tone he said, "I didn't mean to kill the first one, but there was nothing accidental about the second."

A heavy silence fell over the room. I exchanged a look with my parents then Tom. It was a lot to take in. A lot to believe. If Cooper were anyone else I would have dragged my parents out of the room, left him for Tom to deal with for a moment, and returned with an assortment of weapons as backup.

But this was Cooper.

I refused to believe he could hurt anyone. It felt like it needed to be said. "In all the time I've known you, Cooper, I've never seen you hurt anyone. I don't believe this."

He looked around the room as well. "I wish I were the person you think I am."

My father spoke next, "I understand now why you didn't want Tom involved."

Tom let out an audible breath. "I'm going to need more information before I'm able to form an opinion on this."

Cooper looked around at us. "It's a long story."

"But one we need to hear," I said gently.

"If you buried the bodies in Driverton, don't tell me. If you were that stupid, I'd have to arrest you, just on principle," Tom said, joking and serious at the same time. His hand moved to rest on his gun in a message that was clear to all in the room. Tom and Cooper were friends, unless Cooper shared something that made their alliance impossible.

I hugged my arms around myself. I'd missed a number of red flags lately:

My mother's cancer.

My father's drinking.

Please don't let me be wrong about you too, Cooper.

Chapter Fourteen

Cooper

I HAD NO idea where to even start. All of it tangled together and one part was difficult to understand without the others. "My parents were from England, but my siblings and I were born in the United States." I saw the question in her eyes, so I added, "Clay, Collin, Caterina, and me. I was very young when my parents died. I used to remember them, but over time they faded away."

"How did they die?" Tom asked.

"My parents? I was told in a car accident."

Amanda touched my arm lightly. "That must have been so hard."

I hated thinking about that time in my life, but there was no avoiding it anymore. "I've blocked a lot of it out. My uncle took legal custody of Collin, Caterina, and me and sent us off to separate boarding schools. Clay chose to stay in England and live with our grandparents."

Pete frowned. "Separate schools? Why?"

It was a question I'd asked myself many times over the years. "I used to think it was because he hated us, but looking back it made it easier for him to control us. Communication between us was discouraged. He always had a reason why it would be better if we didn't connect. When I was young, I was told Caterina and Collin didn't want to talk to me. Later, I was told they were both going through hard times and keeping them away from me was for my own good. As we got older, Caterina started sneaking away from her school to visit, and she encouraged Collin and me to covertly stay in touch."

Dotty's mouth rounded. "You didn't see each other during the summer? Or holidays?"

"We stayed at the boarding facilities year-round."

Amanda's hand tightened on my arm. "Birthdays?"

"We didn't celebrate them, at least not until Caterina started showing up for them. Those visits were frowned upon, though, and often got us into trouble."

"Trouble?" Tom asked.

"Loss of privileges, confinement to our rooms—whatever successfully discouraged us from doing it again."

Amanda's eyes darkened with sympathy I didn't welcome. "That's so cruel."

"And effective," I added. "I didn't see much of my siblings. Collin and I found secret ways to stay in contact though. We'd call through other people's phones or send emails through their computers. Every move we made was watched. When confronted, the schools claimed the extra security was because people from wealthy families were vulnerable to being kidnapped and they needed to keep us safe. I believed them for a long time and didn't see them for the jailors they were."

Tom's stance relaxed. "Of course you didn't. They were your caretakers. That builds trust even when it shouldn't."

I nodded. "Yes. I understand the runaways who trust the wrong people because they helped them in some way. It's difficult to put people in more than one category—to see them as kind but also dangerous."

Amanda's hand dropped from my arm.

Tom said, "Pete told me two of your siblings died under suspicious circumstances. What happened to them?"

"Shortly after Collin turned eighteen, he called me. He warned me to be careful around our uncle. Collin had gone to a lawyer to see if he could petition for control of his inheritance early and been told that his account was empty. The funds had been dispersed for schooling and large purchases. There were houses we'd never visited, cars we'd never seen, vacations we'd never been on."

"That can't be legal," my father said.

Yeah. "It's not, but Collin dug deeper. Our grandparents retained most of their wealth, so what we were allotted was what had been in the name of our parents. Collin discovered his money had not only been squandered, but had also paid for legal counsel for our uncle."

All eyes, Amanda said, "That must have been scary for you to hear."

"Not really. I was fourteen and Collin had always been both dramatic as well as a little wild. He partied big, talked big, got angry about a lot of things on a regular basis and saw evil where I didn't. You know how you tune out someone sharing a conspiracy theory? I let Collin talk, but it didn't ring true to me. He said our grandparents were evil. Clay was evil. Someone had killed our parents. Our uncle was stealing our money. It was overwhelming; we didn't have the kind of bond that brothers who were raised together have and there was no proof of the money being missing. At least, none tangible enough to convince a young me."

Tom nodded. "What happened to Collin?"

I paused before continuing. This was memory territory I avoided. "He overdosed at a party, one that Caterina attended. Things got ugly fast after that. Caterina spiraled. I was locked down at my school. The funeral was small and quick, supposedly due to the circumstances. Collin was cremated so there was no feeling of closure. By the time Clay and my grandparents showed up, I'd already returned to my school."

In a horrified voice, Amanda asked, "You think your uncle killed him then kept you from seeing the rest of your family?"

I shrugged. "I only know what my uncle said. At that time it was an overdose and neither my grandparents nor Clay wanted to see me."

"Why wouldn't your brother want to see you?" Dotty asked.

"Clay was chasing the money, which was why he chose to go with our grandparents instead of staying with us. The fewer of us there were, the more there would be for him."

"According to your uncle," Tom said.

"Yes."

"Continue," Tom prompted.

I wanted to. Now that I'd opened the door to the past, it needed to come out. "Caterina took Collin's death hard. She stopped coming to see me. My uncle said she was following in Collin's footsteps and the few times I did talk to her she was either drunk or high. He sent her off to a rehab center and I never heard from her again."

"Oh, my God." Amanda looked truly shaken. All I felt was numb.

"About a week before I turned sixteen, my uncle came to my school and took me back to his home. Crazy as it sounds now, I thought it was to celebrate my birthday. I didn't see him often, but he was the only family I had. So, when he told me we needed to fly to England to ask my grandmother for more money, I almost agreed—but I couldn't forget what Collin had told me, so I said no."

Amanda's eyes widened. "And?"

"While alone with him at his house?" Tom asked.

I nodded. "As you can imagine, that didn't go over well." The deeper I went into those memories, the more I felt disconnected from them. I could easily have been retelling what had happened to someone else.

Dotty stepped closer. "What did he do?"

"At first he yelled, then he hit me—a lot. Called me spoiled, ungrateful, weak . . ." My hand went to my face as I remembered the sting of that beating. "No one had ever hit me before. I'd never played a sport. Given a free afternoon, I'd always preferred to read. I was weak—"

"You were *a child*," Amanda said in a rush.

She might have sympathy for who I was back then, but I

didn't. "His goal was to get me to obey, but it did the opposite. The more he hurt me, the more I remembered and began to believe the things Collin had said about him. So, I told my uncle I knew he'd spent our money and he wouldn't get a penny more of it."

"No," Tom said.

"I was too young to understand how foolish that was." I didn't want the sympathy I saw in the eyes of Amanda and her family. Would they feel as sorry for me at the end of my story? I doubted it. "When I didn't back down, my uncle threatened to do to me what our family did to everyone who stood in their way. He laughed and asked if I knew why I hadn't heard from Caterina. He said it was because he'd dealt with her just like he had Collin, just like he had my parents."

Tom made a sound deep in his throat. "Did he say he'd killed them?"

"He implied it. Honestly, I was dazed, scared, bloody . . . a lot of that night is a blur now. All I know is that he grabbed me, lifted me off my feet, and started carrying me out of the room. I kicked and yelled, but he was a large man and I didn't have the strength to fight him. I don't know where we were headed or what he intended to do, but I was scared and I knew I couldn't stop him. I grabbed a statue from a shelf we passed and bashed it into the back of his head as hard as I could."

Amanda gasped.

I continued, "We both fell to the floor. I stood up. He didn't. He just lay there with blood pooling behind his head and his eyes open. I'll never forget that moment because it haunts me, especially at night."

"Did you call anyone?" Tom asked. "Do anything?"

"I ran." I grunted with disgust at who I'd been back then.

"Anyone would have," Amanda said.

I couldn't meet her gaze. "I didn't know what else to do so I slept outside the first night. I was naïve enough to believe that if I made it back to my school I'd be able to find someone who would help me. A couple saw me walking on the road and offered me a ride."

"You didn't." Tom knew where this was going. We'd tracked enough kidnapped children to have come across this method too many times. If a perp could get a child into their car, the outcome was rarely a good one. Even when I found the child alive, often enough damage was done I wondered if they'd ever recover. "Yeah, that was another bad choice. They offered me a bottle of water. I gulped it down and woke up, feet and hands bound, in a room with a couple of boys my age. Neither of them was covered with their own blood as I was, but they were just as scared. One of them told me not to eat or drink anything that was brought because it was always drugged."

Amanda slid beneath my arm and hugged me. I felt her and didn't at the same time. My body was still in the present, but my mind was reliving a day I'd worked hard to forget. The stench of urine, the pain throbbing through me. Fear so vivid I could almost taste it.

I couldn't stop yet. "They said there'd been another boy,

but he'd been taken and not returned. Something in me snapped. I went from being scared to crazy angry. There was no way I'd survived my uncle to be killed by whoever had taken me. I was super skinny at the time and was able to free my hands, then my feet, then the other two boys. I had nothing but rope and fury. When the man who had taken me walked in the room, I jumped him from behind. I tried and failed to strangle him, but it was enough of a fight that I was able to grab his gun."

Amanda shivered against me. I held her close without looking down at her. "I knew next to nothing about guns. Had never touched one in my life. I held it up between us and told him to get the fuck away from us. My hands were shaking so much I'm surprised he didn't just take the gun."

No one moved or spoke as I took a breath.

"He sneered at me and said I couldn't do it—that I wasn't a killer. He was wrong. I unloaded all the bullets into his chest, even after he'd fallen at my feet. I kept shooting. The other two boys ran out the door and I stood there looking at him for a long time. I'd killed another man. The woman came running in and fell to her knees next to him. I watched her cry and felt nothing."

Amanda hugged me tighter. "Cooper, you were in shock."

That was probably true, but it was more than that. "A piece of me died that day, a piece that doesn't come back."

Amanda brought a hand to my cheek. "That's not true, Cooper. And you're not a murderer. You were defending yourself."

"Both sound like self-defense to me," Tom added.

Pete said, "You did what you had to."

I shook my head. "No, I did so much less than I should have. I didn't stay to make sure the other kids were okay. I didn't check the other rooms to free anyone else who might have been there. I ran—again. And this time I kept running. I knew there was no going back to my old life so I didn't try to. I just kept moving, for weeks I think, stealing what I needed, sleeping in any warm, dry place I could find. Driverton looked as good as any other town and the hardware store was easy enough to break into."

"Until you met my father," Amanda said softly.

"And his fist." It was meant to be a joke but it missed that mark.

Pete said, "I hate that I hit you. Especially after everything you'd been through."

"You had to protect yourself." That day was also still painfully easy to remember. "You walked in and I felt trapped. I hit you first."

Pete's eyes shone with emotion. "I knew something bad had happened to you. The look in your eyes, I'd seen it before, but only when I served in the Army. People come back different. When you started crying, I recognized it as due to something much worse than the pain I'd inflicted."

"I still can't believe you offered me a place to stay and a job."

Amanda tipped her head back to look at me. "I can. I saw you that night, Cooper. The man you are today would have offered the boy you were back then a place to stay too.

You were covered with old bruises. Your clothing was filthy and torn. You needed help and we all recognized that."

As I returned to the moment, I realized I was holding onto Amanda as tightly as she was holding me. It felt so damn good, and excruciatingly wrong. I released her and stepped back. "You did help me. All of you."

Tom cut in, "Your uncle's death should have been a high-profile case, but I don't remember ever hearing about it. Are you sure you killed him?"

"He was definitely dead."

"I've also never heard about a Cooper Landon going missing. That should have been a missing person's report sent to every police department."

I'd thought of that over the years as well. "Unless my family didn't want me found. My grandparents are both gone now. There's only one Landon left. He's either a lucky bastard or as evil as my uncle was."

Pete nodded. "You want to confront him."

"The alternative is to wait for him to make a move and I can't risk that he'd come here looking for me." I glanced at Amanda. "I won't risk that."

"I'd hold off on having any genetic testing done until we find out how involved your brother was in what happened to you," Tom said.

"I'm done hiding. Amanda said the treatment is time sensitive. I'm not waiting."

Amanda opened her mouth to say something but seemed to change her mind. When our eyes met again, I could see the conflict battling in her. She wanted me safe, but our baby needed answers only I could provide. I understood the struggle because for me there could be no us until I knew I'd done everything I could to protect her. I held her gaze and said, "I'm driving to the lab today."

"I'm going with you."

Hours alone with her when it was already nearly impossible to keep my hands off her? No, I needed to stay clearheaded. "I'm not planning on returning. At least, not until I have some answers."

None of the others were fighting to come with me or jumping in to say I should stay. I understood that as well. It was one thing to suspect I'd robbed and lied, but another thing entirely to hear I had the blood of two men on my hands. It confirmed what some people only suspected about themselves: I was capable of taking another life.

"I don't like your plan," Tom said.

"Forget you know anything about it." His feelings on the matter wouldn't stop me.

Pete shook his head and stepped closer. "If there is one thing the military taught me it was to take a moment to reassess a situation when someone in my unit suggests that happen. Rushing into action without a good plan only works in the movies."

My hands fisted at my side. "I need to face my brother head-on."

"And then what?" Pete asked. "You said you don't know his character. You could be walking into anything."

"That's my risk to take."

"Is it?" Pete countered. "If the only one you're considering is yourself, I suppose it is. I was under the impression, though, that there was more to you than that."

I threw my hands up in the air. "I'll do whatever I need to do to keep this town safe from my problems."

"Because?" Pete pushed.

The truth burst out of me. "Because alone is how I've always been, how I always will be. I'm not one of you—"

"I'm offended," Tom cut in.

Dotty added, "That's not how I ever saw you, Cooper."

"Me neither," Amanda said from my side.

Pete's tone turned stern. "Son, I'm going to help you here. The feeling that you're on the outside looking in? That there's no one you can truly trust? That's PTSD. Those memories you keep trying to block out? They don't go away just because you ignore them. They're part of you now—"

Temper rising, I cut him off. "What do you want from me? I'm trying to keep you safe."

"No, Cooper," Pete said, "you're trying to keep yourself safe. You're less afraid of your brother killing you than you are of trusting us to be on your side. I understand why, but you're wrong. You might not have had anyone before you came to Driverton, but look around. Do any of us look scared? Or do we look the opposite? You should know by now that if someone comes for one of us, they come for all of us—and you *are* one of us."

A wave of emotion made it temporarily difficult for me to speak. Amanda's hand taking mine was welcome support. I didn't see myself as being afraid of anything, but was the numbness I felt on most days a choice? Like anger? What would I feel if I didn't choose it? "Even knowing what I've done?"

Pete's face tightened. He glanced at Dotty and Amanda before addressing me again. "When I left the Army, I was a heavy drinker. It was the only way I could shut out certain images. War is an ugly thing, son. I made choices, followed orders I felt I had to—but were they right? I'll never know. I've looked a man straight in the eye and ended his life. I've taken out targets only to discover there were civilians in the area. One was a family of five who sought shelter from a rainstorm. The youngest wasn't even a year old. Legally I was innocent because the intel was wrong. Does that make it easier for me to look myself in the mirror? No. I know what I did and I carry the weight of it every day."

The self-loathing in Pete's eyes was a feeling that was familiar to me. I didn't bother to tell him it hadn't been his fault because I knew that didn't matter. The circumstances around why I'd killed had never made those memories easier for me.

Pete continued, "My question for you is: Do you think I'm a good man? You've seen me as a husband, father, friend . . . Do I merit the support of the town?"

"Yes," I said to all of it without hesitation.

"Don't judge yourself more harshly than you judge me. And don't dismiss us when we say we should handle this together." Pete returned and put an arm around Dotty again. "Dotty never let me get away with that."

Dotty smiled up at Pete. "Damn right I didn't."

Amanda gave my hand a squeeze. "So, what would be a

better plan?"

I met her gaze and, for a moment, lost myself in the strength I saw there. Pete was right, she didn't look afraid. None of them did. "If I took you with me to the lab today?"

Tom added, "Then came back and gave us time to investigate this brother of yours. Everette has a cousin in the FBI. We can reach out to him."

"You really think it's wise to bring that kind of attention to me after what I shared?" I asked.

Tom raised and lowered a shoulder. "The first one is a puzzle I think we'll find a lot of answers in when we solve. The second one would be a cold case by now. Even if you're linked to it somehow, you'd be considered one of the victims from that day. Something doesn't sit right with me about that case either. They would have tracked down the boys you set free. Someone would have mentioned you. Did the investigation not find any DNA on the ropes you said they'd bound you with? Why did no one look for you? That's where I suggest we start."

I took a moment to study each of their expressions and all I saw was the same grit I admired in Amanda. "And if we discover my brother played a role in what happened?"

Tom stood straighter. "Then we call in favors and gather our resources."

I shook my head. "Going up against someone with as much money as my brother has isn't something we could do legally. None of you can be involved in what I might have to do."

"That's not your decision to make," Amanda said firmly.

When I looked at her, she placed her free hand over her stomach. "I'm fully invested in how this turns out."

Dotty added, "We all are."

Tom made a sound akin to a growl. "There aren't too many things I'd risk my pension for, but I'd turn in my gun and badge before I'd let you face Clay alone. Cooper, you, and I have done some shady shit to save strangers. Do you honestly believe I'd do less for you?"

It was an incredibly humbling moment. I'd revealed my ugliest secrets and the Glenfords were still there, ready to go to battle with and for me. Amanda was at my side without a promise of a relationship. Tom was willing to risk his future security to help me. I didn't know what to do with all the emotions rushing through me.

I'd always told myself they accepted me because they didn't know the real me. What if I'd been wrong? What if I really was part of this family?

Amanda and I were still holding hands. My chests tightened painfully. I didn't deserve someone like her in my life, but I vowed right then that I would become someone who would. "If we're going to get to Bangor before the lab closes, we'd better get going."

"We?" Amanda asked in a husky voice.

It didn't feel like the time or the place to tell her how I felt so I released her hand but softened the move with a wink. "Unless you think I should take Tom instead."

Chapter Fifteen

Amanda

A SHORT TIME later Cooper and I were in my car heading to Bangor. We'd chosen my vehicle because it was more comfortable than his truck, and I could have insisted on driving, but I understood that he needed to regain some sense of being in control.

When my father had said that Cooper was less afraid of getting killed than he was of trusting us to be on his side, it changed the way I'd looked at all the times Cooper had closed me out. Keeping a distance might not have been a sign he didn't care—it might have been the opposite. The Cooper beside me, the one willing to risk his safety for the sake of our baby, was the Cooper I knew.

My heart ached for him each time I thought about everything he'd been through before he came to Driverton. From the early loss of his parents and the deliberate isolation he'd endured to what it must have been like for a child to be forced to violently defend himself against adults. It was no wonder Cooper had trust issues.

My parents' unwavering support of him didn't surprise

me. He might look at them and only see how much they'd done for him, but it was obvious that he'd done just as much for them. The same could be said about him and Tom. My guess was that if Everette, Levi, or Ollie had been in the mix earlier they would have stood with Cooper as well. Ten years of taking care of them as well. Cooper wasn't fooling anyone. He cared about everyone a lot more than he said. He didn't want to leave.

What I didn't know was if that meant he cared about me the same way he cared about my parents, Tom, and others . . . or if we had something spe—

I stopped myself there with a groan. This was where our friendship train repeatedly derailed. Why couldn't I accept that we didn't have more? I would have blamed the baby, but the truth was I'd always wanted more from him. "Thank you for doing this, Cooper."

He frowned then shot a glance at me. "There was no chance I wouldn't. My only question was if it could be done without linking it to my real name."

"I understand that now. I'm sorry about the things I said."

He glanced at me again before returning his eyes to the road. "You have nothing to be sorry about."

That wasn't entirely true. "If I hadn't gone to you the night I learned that my mother had cancer—"

"Don't regret that. I don't."

I inhaled deeply. "You say that—"

"Because it's true. Amanda, I have no idea how any of this is going to turn out, but if I had to accidentally make a baby with someone, there's no one I'd rather make one with."

Was he serious? It felt like he was trying to cheer me up, but I wasn't sure. "Are you trying to be funny?"

He made a show of debating that with himself. I loved the slight smile that curled his lips. "Trying? It's not a well-known fact, but I'm secretly fucking hilarious."

I turned in my seat to face him better. "Really?" Tapping a finger on my chin, I said, "Tell me a joke."

"You doubt my skills?"

I tipped my chin upward and folded my hands on my lap. "Not in everything, but in the humor department, yes."

That made him smile. "I suppose I should thank you for the first part." After a moment, he asked, "Do you know why I've always been popular at nudist events?"

"Nudist events?" I asked to stall. Images of him naked were flashing through my head, warming my cheeks. There was nothing amusing about how easily he could send my thoughts straight to the gutter. How was I supposed to concentrate on anything when all I could think about was how talented he was with his hands, his tongue, the way he moved inside me?

He cocked his head to the side in mock pride. "I'm the only one who can carry two trays of drinks and a dozen donuts."

It took me a second to get the joke, but then I bit back a laugh. "Remind me not to ask you to bring me a donut."

He pressed his lips together. "You're a tough one. Hang on, I have another joke. Did you hear about the constipated mathematician with a broken calculator?"

"No."

"He had to work it out with a pencil."

I did laugh at that. "Oh, my God, that's disgusting."

"But funny."

"Is it, though?" My smile widened.

"You think you could do better? Bring it on."

Jokes weren't my thing, but I remembered one a graphic designer had told to break the ice before a meeting. "The dating pool in the city is a little shallow. I've had to lower my standards. Recently I started dating a spider. It's not so bad. We have a lot in common. He's a web designer."

Cooper groaned, but smiled. "Work jokes?"

"Dick jokes?"

"Touché." He raised a hand. "One last one. What should you say to a butt cheek if it starts bragging?"

I laughed. "I don't know this one, but I feel like you would say: 'You're full of shit'?"

"You've heard the joke!"

"I didn't. I swear. I'm just in your head with you."

"Don't look around. It's scary up there."

We shared a laugh and I said, "I'm not used to seeing you like this."

"Joking around?"

"And laughing."

His expression sobered and he took a moment before answering. "Considering everything that's going on and all the unknowns, this will probably sound crazy, but I feel like a huge weight has been lifted off me."

"That doesn't sound crazy at all. You've been pretending to be someone else for a decade. You can finally be yourself. That must feel freeing."

He nodded. "It does. How do you always know how I feel even when I'm still figuring it out for myself?"

"We're not exactly strangers." I spontaneously laid my hand on his leg.

"No, we're not." He glanced down at his thigh then back at the road. The flush that reddened his neck and cheeks was so damn sexy I wanted to kiss every inch of him I'd just warmed.

What did he feel toward me? He was attracted enough to sleep with me, but was it more than that? Was he the type who found a majority of women attractive enough to have sex with? As soon as I imagined it, I hated the idea of him with another woman.

"Hey, hey, hey," he said as he put his hand over mine. "Those little fingers of yours have quite a pinch to them."

What? Only then did I realize I'd clenched my hand on his skin. "Sorry. I didn't realize . . ." I loosened my hold and went to remove my hand, but he held it there.

"You were picturing me with someone else, weren't you?"

My hand shook beneath his. "Maybe."

His fingers laced with mine. "I hate the idea of you with someone else too."

That's all it took for me to start to melt for him.

Oh, no. I refuse to throw myself at him again.

"You know, I blame you for why I was a virgin until I

went to college," I blurted out.

We both froze.

Don't say more. Stop.

I added, "I used to have a serious thing for you."

"I know," he said, and embarrassment flooded in.

I tried once again to tug my hand free, but with even less success. Anger replaced embarrassment. "Is this some kind of game to you? If so, it's not one I enjoy."

He released my hand. I returned to sitting back, facing forward in my seat and he asked, "What are you upset about?"

"What am I . . .?" I folded my arms across my chest. "I don't want to fight with you. We're getting along and that's good."

"It is good."

"For the baby's sake, it's important."

"I agree."

"Good."

"Are you angry with me?"

"No," I snapped. I was angry with myself. Everything would have been easier if I could relax and accept that we were only friends. Friend's who'd had sex, but nothing more.

After a moment, he said, "You sound angry. If I said something that upset you . . ."

"Could we not talk about it?" I took a deep breath and began to calm. I'm not proud of the excuse I tossed at him, but it was the best I could come up with. "I'm going to be emotional—I'm pregnant."

"Oh." After a pause, he added, "I thought it was because

I didn't say that I used to have a serious thing for you too. Because I did. I thought that went without having to be said."

And, whoosh, I was completely confused again. "You used to have a thing for me?"

"It wasn't obvious in the way I always showed up wherever you were?"

"I thought you were watching over me . . . making sure I was safe."

"That too." He smiled.

I handed another piece of my heart to him right then and there. "If you were into me, what happened the night of my prom? You couldn't get me out of your car fast enough."

He made a sound deep in his chest. "You were Pete's daughter and I respected that."

"I was so angry when you told me you'd taken me only because my father asked you to."

"I thought it was better if you were angry."

"Better? For who? Me or you?"

"Both. You needed to go to college. Everyone knew you had dreams that were bigger than Driverton. I couldn't hold you back or go with you. You deserved your chance to fly— and you did. Your success is a frequent topic in town."

I took a moment to digest that. "It was important to me to prove myself."

"I know."

"It's not as important now. I love what I do and I'll continue to work from Driverton, but my reasons have changed. I want my own house to raise my baby in and to be able to care for my parents as they age. I don't need more than that."

"I don't have any money saved—"

"I do." I couldn't judge Cooper for not saving because I knew where his money had gone and that was back into the community. Ollie's restaurant had a new roof and Ollie was only one of many Cooper had helped. "I'm thinking about buying the Stanley house. It's big and needs work, but nothing that can't be fixed."

"I might know a handyman who could help you out."

"You do?"

"I do."

We drove a bit without talking, then I said, "I'm going to begin to show soon. People already think we're a couple. We may want to explain to them that we're just friends."

He didn't answer at first. In fact, it took him so long to answer I was beginning to question if he'd heard me. "Or we could go on a date."

I gulped. I would have said something, but I was too afraid of blurting out something that would cause him to pull back again.

He continued, "I'd like to take you out."

"On a date?"

"Yeah. You had those in the city, didn't you? I pick you up. We go to dinner. Maybe a walk afterward. Talk."

"Talk?" Why was I parroting everything he said?

"I don't know what you're thinking, but if it's anything like what I think about whenever we're together, it's probably not a good idea. I need to figure out if my brother is a risk, and I'm having a hard enough time concentrating with you around."

I reached out and traced a finger a few inches up his thigh. "So this would be a problem?"

His voice was a little strangled and evidence of his arousal began to strain impressively against the front of his jeans. "From the first time I laid eyes on you I knew you'd be trouble."

I traced just a little higher. "So I should stop?"

He groaned, took my hand in his, and placed it on his bulge. "Being able to think is overrated."

Chapter Sixteen

Cooper

IT'S AMAZING HOW fast a man can change his mind when the woman he loves has her hand on his cock. I pulled off the highway, parked at a mid-rate hotel, nearly sprinted with her to check in, and by some miracle found our room without hardly ever taking my eyes off her.

I opened the door, lifted her in my arms, then kicked it closed behind me and carried her across the room to the bed. I told myself to take it slowly, be gentle. She destroyed that plan by ripping at my clothing impatiently. Whatever restraint I had fell away with our clothing. Naked, she wrapped her legs around my waist and I moved to brace her back against the nearest wall.

Our kisses were deep and demanding. Our hands explored and excited. I ran the tip of my cock back and forth against her wet sex, holding back my pleasure the best I could. I bent her backward over my arm to love each of her breasts in turn, not gently as I had the first time. This was a rough claiming that had her moaning in the most delicious way.

She did this little move with her hips that brought the tip of my cock to her ready center and I entered her with a powerful thrust. We both went wild after that. She clung to me, meeting each deep thrust with one of her own, taking me deeper and deeper.

I lost myself in her kiss again, in the feel of her all around. This was my woman. I drove into her again and again, powerfully, ruthlessly, taking what I'd told myself should wait.

The way she moved with me, the pleased sound she made, was all the encouragement I needed to let myself go. I took her against the wall, against the back of the couch, then turned her over and took her from behind while she was bent over the desk.

I took her with all the passion I'd held in check over the years. This wasn't fucking. It wasn't lovemaking. This was something more primal and somehow more meaningful.

I laced my hands with hers, as I pounded into her, loving how she arched her back and matched my rhythm. Only when her fingers clenched mine and she shuddered, did I let myself join her in release. I kissed a trail down her neck, released her hands, and continued to kiss my way down her back.

Never in my life had I seen a more perfect ass and the smile she shot me over her shoulder was pure sex. She moved to straighten, but with a firm hand I held her in place then slid a finger into her and pumped in and out slowly while seeking her clit with my thumb. As she relaxed I slipped another finger inside her and did a little swirl around until I found the spot that made her beg me not to stop.

I loved the way her hot, wet sex tightened around my fingers as if trying to pull me deeper. With the initial urgency sated, I took my time to learn the secrets to her pleasure. I nibbled and kissed, teased, and explored. As her excitement rose, my cock did as well.

"Turn around," I commanded, sliding my fingers out.

She did.

"Get up on the bed."

She crawled onto it, then lay back. I pulled her forward, hand light on her stomach, and drove into her again. Her eyes never left mine as I ever so slowly dipped deeply into her then pulled out, enjoying her with more control this time.

She spread her legs wider and gripped the edge of the bed with both hands. I lifted her ass and drove deeper. She bit her bottom lip then said, "Harder, Cooper. I love it hard and fast." She didn't need to say that twice.

We mated with a wildness that left us both sweaty, breathless, and coming for a second time. I withdrew then laid her gently farther up on the bed. A moment later, I returned with a warm towel and cleaned her. Caring for her was a different but equally moving kind of pleasure.

I half expected her to lift the blankets and slide beneath them, but instead she sat up and ran a hand through her hair. "We need to get going or the lab will close."

I looked at the clock near the bed and told her, "You're right."

She shimmied off the bed. "If we go now we can make it."

I started gathering our clothing off the floor then threw her underwear at her and joked, "This is your fault, Handsy-Mc-Handster."

Smiling, she stepped into her panties then grabbed her bra out of my hands. "We're name calling now, Mr. I-Drive-Over-Grass-Medians-When-I-See-a-Hotel?"

I laughed. "It was an emergency."

She chuckled, leaned forward, and kissed me before pulling her shirt on. "It did feel like one."

I dressed as quickly as I could then helped her finish. "Let's go."

A short time later I was seated beside Amanda in the waiting room of the lab. I was poised to fill out the paperwork a receptionist had handed me on a clipboard but as I read it over, my hand began to shake.

Amanda put a hand on my leg. "What's wrong?"

I wouldn't have answered anyone else, but I didn't want to block Amanda out anymore.

"The appointment was made under Cooper Davis. I'll have to use my fake name."

"Is that a problem? We told them you don't have health insurance. All they'll do is bill us . . . you."

I couldn't sort through how I was feeling enough to articulate it to Amanda. "I don't want to be Cooper Davis anymore, but I have no proof that I'm Cooper Landon."

She searched my face, then stood. "Give me a minute." She walked over to the receptionist. When Amanda returned, she was smiling. "It's fine. You can use your real name and they will bill us for the testing. I told her Davis was your middle name and that you'd lost your wallet. I explained how time sensitive this is and she was willing to send the sample on without your ID as long as we mail her a copy of your license as soon as it comes in."

When she sat beside me again, I leaned over and kissed her cheek. "You're amazing. I hope you realize that."

"Thank you." She blushed but smiled. "All I did was try to see things from her perspective. She has a job to do. I knew if I made it easy for her to help us she would. Who doesn't want to save a baby's life?"

"I've seen too much to have that kind of faith in humanity."

"Then look again. I'm not saying there aren't bad people in the world. But if you trust that it's there, there's more good than evil."

"If you say so."

"You think my dad is a good person."

"Of course."

"Me? Tom?"

"You know I do."

"Ollie, Everette, Levi—"

The moment quickly became too intense to be comfortable in public. I looked away. "You're the exceptions."

She gave my leg a light squeeze. "Or you've surrounded yourself with good people because you're smarter than you give yourself credit for."

I turned back to face her and she smiled up at me. "You think you have me figured out?"

"I'm beginning to."

Considering how confused I was lately, that was possible. "And what have you determined?"

Her smile turned gentle. "You take care of people the way you wish someone had taken care of you. You've lived two totally different lives so sometimes it feels like you're two people and that's why you're struggling with that form. It feels like you're choosing one over the other and you're not sure what that will mean as far as who you are."

"It sounds like you understand how that feels."

"I do. I went to the city and tried to become someone else. I wanted to be—more, I guess. I wasn't happy though. Now I'm home, and trying to figure how I fit in and if I still do."

"Everyone I talk to in town adores you."

"But they don't know me. Not anymore. I feel like I'm starting over."

"Yes." I looked from her to the still blank form. I thought about the young boy who'd run to Driverton. I didn't want to be him, but I also didn't want to be the man who'd left him behind. I was done accepting being invisible as a way of life. "I'm starting over too." Writing Cooper Landon felt like I was signing a contract with myself. There was no going back. I filled in only what was necessary on the form then returned it to the desk.

A lab tech came to the door of the waiting room and called my name. I rose to my feet and followed her into the other room as I mulled over the name Amanda had fabricated for me: Cooper Davis Landon.

Not one or the other.

Someone new, based on both but held back by neither.

The act of giving a blood sample was quick and uncomplicated. I was back with Amanda a few minutes later with a Band-Aid on the crook of my arm and a strong desire to have Amanda all to myself again. As we walked to the car together, I said, "We could easily make it back to Driverton tonight or . . ."

Her eyes widened and she smiled. "We did pay for the room for the night."

"It'd be a shame to waste it."

Her hands went to her cheeks. "I could tell my parents we didn't want to drive back in the dark."

"It's not like you can get more pregnant."

She laughed at that. "You're such an ass."

I spun her then pulled her flush against me. "But am I an ass you want to sleep with tonight?"

She arched and wound her arms around my neck. "Is this where I'm supposed to play hard to get?"

I bent and growled in her ear, "No, that's later, when we're both naked and you pretend you don't want me to catch you as we sprint around the bed."

All smiles, she said, "That does actually sound like a much better time to do it."

Chapter Seventeen

Amanda

THE NEXT MORNING, showered and dressed in the same clothes I'd worn the day before, I put a lid on the tea I'd just poured myself in the lobby of the hotel. Cooper was debating his choice of pastry from the breakfast bar. Our eyes met and I said, "I don't want to go back yet."

He held my gaze. "I understand that feeling too well, but I can't move forward with anything . . . not my life . . . not you, until I figure out the situation with my brother."

Inspecting the pastry options was safer than letting him see the disappointment I was afraid would show in my eyes. I'd never felt closer to Cooper than I had when I woke up in his arms that morning. We'd showered together, laughed about noises we'd heard through the walls during the night. It hadn't sounded like a couple having sex—more like a family of raccoons knocking everything over. Whether they were drunk or sexually adventurous, we'd done our best to match their enthusiasm. I'd never look at a hotel desk the same way again.

So how had Cooper and I become awkward around each

other again? He hadn't made any promises or declared feelings for me. In fact, his original plan had been to take me to dinner and see how that went.

If I didn't want to be on this roller coaster, why did I keep hopping back on? The truth was almost as scary as being pregnant. Being with Cooper on his terms and when both of our lives were upside down felt better than anything I'd experienced with another man. I didn't want a man who'd say all the right things but leave as soon as things got hard. Cooper might not be ready for a normal relationship yet, but he'd just come out of hiding for our baby.

Flowers and pretty words could never top something like that.

Still, it didn't make the place we were in easier. I wanted to tell him he didn't have to look for his brother. It was so tempting to suggest that after the baby was safe we could run away, choose different names, and hide out together.

I had my parents to think of—so tempting or not, that wasn't an option.

I doubted Cooper would ever go back into hiding again anyway. He was already walking taller, looking more people directly in the eye. Like a man preparing for battle? I couldn't bear the thought of losing him, but I had no idea how to protect him.

"You okay?" he asked as I took a long time making my selection.

I grabbed one of the individually wrapped muffins. "Yes."

He guided me away from the food to a booth. I slid into

one side, he took the other. "When we get back to Driver-ton, things might happen fast. I'm hoping Tom did some digging into my family. If he didn't, I'll do my own research. Mine involves leaving, though . . ."

"With Tom?"

"Or on my own. I know how to travel fast and light. I'm very good at getting people to talk as well as give me access to places."

I could see that. Cooper gave off a vibe that he could be trusted. "I want to go with you."

He shook his head. "There's no way I'd put you and the baby at risk."

"What about how I feel about you putting yourself at risk?" He frowned as if that was something he hadn't consid-ered so I continued, "I am terrified that something will happen to you. I don't want to lose you." There, I'd said it.

He didn't say I wouldn't.

He didn't say anything.

The words "I love you" were on the tip of my tongue, but saying them would have been a selfish choice. He wasn't ready and I wasn't ready to say them and not hear them in return.

After a few minutes, he reached out and took my hand in his. "I'll be as careful as I can be. I don't want you to lose me either." His eyes lit with humor when he said that last part.

I reluctantly smiled in response. "What am I going to do with you?"

The smile he shot me was all sex. "I have several ideas, but most should wait." His expression sobered and he said,

"We've done this all backward." He turned my hand over in his. "How does it not feel wrong?"

My heart started wildly beating in my chest. Had he really just said that? "Because it's not?"

"You've definitely complicated things, Amanda. All this stuff with my family would have been a lot easier if I didn't care what happened to me. When I'm with you I start believing crazy things like all of this can work out."

I gripped his hand tight. "It can."

Memories darkened his eyes. "It's been so long since I believed in anything. When I was young, I believed if I was good, good things would happen for me. I quickly learned that wasn't true. Then I thought if I fought hard enough, I could win, but that wasn't true either. I don't have a good track record when it comes to winning."

"No." He let me glimpse his pain so clearly, I felt as if it were my own. His view of himself was understandable and my fears were only playing on his own negative view of himself. He needed me to believe in him. "How many children have you rescued? I bet they don't see you the way you do. Their parents don't care what you did at sixteen, they met the man you became because of that, and he's a hero."

Cooper blinked a few times quickly. He brought my hand up to his mouth for a quick kiss. "My family won't win this time."

Not knowing what that would entail scared me, but I kept that to myself and prayed Tom would have some good news for Cooper. "Maybe your uncle was the source of all your trouble. Maybe you're free."

He let out an audible breath. "That would change everything."

I nodded even as I prayed that that possibility also led to us being together. Was it too much to ask for some kind of sign that things would work out?

"Your nose is bleeding again," Cooper said gently as he handed me a tissue.

I held the tissue below my nose and glared upward. *I see you also have a sense of humor.* Thankfully it only required a few dabs to clear up. Still, it was embarrassing. I looked away and said, "When it comes to being sexy, I'm nailing it."

"Amanda, do you think a bloody nose could make me forget how beautiful you are—inside and out?" I was warming all over from that comment when he added, "I've seen you look much worse."

That had my attention snapping back to him. The smile in his eyes was all that saved him. Besides, he did have a point. "Are you referring to the first time I tried grain alcohol shots and threw up all over myself?"

His grin was telling. "You were angry with me for seeing you like that, then angrier when I used a garden hose to wash you off."

"It was rude."

"You didn't see yourself. There was no way you were getting into my truck like that."

I groaned.

He chuckled. "Vivid as that experience still is in my head, I was actually referring to the time you volunteered to help the school clear the walking trails and ended up with poison ivy all over your face."

"I wish that was the only place I'd had it. That's when I learned the importance of using dish detergent instead of regular soap. My skin softening bar spread that oil all over—and by that I mean all over. If you think my face looked bad you should have seen my bits and pieces. To this day if I so much as look at a three leafed plant my crotch itches."

"That may be the one time I can say I'm glad we weren't on intimate terms."

I laughed. "It was so bad. My parents had to drive me to Bangor because even my regular gynecologist didn't want to see it. The hospital said it was one of the worst cases they'd ever seen. I've always been an overachiever."

We were both sitting there with big smiles, just enjoying the moment. "Would you think I'm crazy if I said I've enjoyed today?"

"No, I was thinking that I should get you pregnant on a regular basis so we can do this more often." He said it with a straight face that he couldn't maintain when I balled up and threw a napkin at him.

We shared a laugh.

When we sobered, he added, "Seriously, I'm normally a miserable bastard. This was a good day."

"It was, which might be proof that we're both nuts."

His eyes sparkled with laughter. "At least we're not the only ones. I don't know a sane person in Driverton."

"You think it's something in the water?" I started laughing again, this time so hard my eyes started to water.

"Must be. Lunatics, every last one of us."

Us. Was he finally beginning to see himself as belonging? I inhaled sharply then said, "And yet it's the only place I can imagine raising my children."

Children? Was I testing if the idea would send him running? I felt crazy because we had yet to go on an official date, but I still held my breath as I waited for his response.

He took a moment then said, "Me too."

We weren't at the promise stage. I knew he had issues he wanted to address before he could move forward with anything, but I'd needed to know what was possible. For where we were and what we were facing, his answer and the way he took my hand in his was enough.

Chapter Eighteen

Bradford

"I'M HEADING TO Driverton, Maine," Bradford Wilson said in a curt tone to Ian Barrington.

"I thought you were in Brazil."

"I was and that put a new spin on my search for Cooper."

"In what way?"

"I'm beginning to understand why no one looked too hard for the uncle, Ryssen Landon. He's buried in a tomb outside of Sao Paulo where he's been for the last decade."

"Clay said his body was never found."

"Clay said a lot of things that don't hold up against what I'm finding. It's definitely Ryssen. I had the body tested."

"Of course you did. You're remaining under the radar with all of this, right? Clay is too closely linked to my family for this to play out in the media."

"You don't think I know that? This has the potential of being a legal mess. Ryssen had the back of his head bashed in. Someone murdered him."

"Shit."

"And gave him a nice burial then pretended he was still missing for another year before he was declared dead."

"Clay has his faults, but I can't imagine him doing that."

"Money brings out the devil in people, but I'm not saying Clay did it. What I'm saying is that Clay's version is either an outright lie or an implausible story he was fed and accepted. I find it very interesting that there was never an official missing person's report on either Ryssen or Cooper."

"A lot went down in my own family that was never addressed legally." Ian sighed. "I understand how a question can be so painful to ask, it's easier to accept a more palatable story. We wouldn't have Kade back if it weren't for my aunt's journal. Clay thought Caterina and Cooper wanted nothing to do with him. I'm sure he didn't look very hard."

Bradford groaned. "This is different. Kade didn't know you existed. Cooper doesn't want to be found."

"Hold on. The last time we talked, you doubted Cooper was still alive. What changed?"

"Cooper Landon had genetic testing in Bangor, Maine. Surveillance cameras show him entering and leaving a medical building with a woman."

"Have you been using the CIA's databases again?"

"Why have access to them if we're not going to use them?"

"Be careful. We don't want to bring attention to any of this."

"I know how to cover my digital tracks. You worry too much."

"Because you don't worry at all."

Bradford laughed without humor. "True enough."

Always the first to refocus, Ian circled back to the heart of the matter. "What was Cooper tested for?"

"Festner's disease. It's one of the causes of sudden infant death. His lady friend might be more than a friend."

"What else did you learn?"

"Facial recognition showed hits for him in the area for years but the name linked to his driver's license is Cooper Davis, a resident of an extremely small town in the middle of nowhere."

"What the hell is he doing up in Maine?"

"Hiding better than most war criminals, and I'm beginning to understand why. Someone was trimming the Landon family tree. Clay's parents died in a car accident that was never investigated. I'm not big on conspiracies, but there was a lot of death in that family in a relatively short period of time. Clay's parents, his uncle, his older brother, both of Clay's grandparents."

"You think Clay was involved?"

"His timeline doesn't match what I found in Brazil. According to Clay, Ryssen flew to England, had an argument with his mother, Clay's grandmother, about money. Ryssen returned home, picked up Cooper, withdrew him from school via an email a couple of days later, and sent someone to retrieve his things. The problem is—Ryssen couldn't have sent that email because he was already dead and buried."

"Someone didn't want anyone looking for the uncle or Cooper."

"Exactly. Caterina was still essentially on the run herself.

I don't see a motivation for her. If she was after money she would have sought Clay out sooner."

"You think Clay killed his uncle? Then covered it up?"

"Clay, his grandmother, Cooper. Someone killed Ryssen and flew his body to Brazil. I don't consider myself a paranoid man, but if Clay is systematically wiping out his family, I'd rather not hand him his only brother."

"I'm trying to imagine Clay orchestrating something like that and I can't." Ian let out a low whistle. "But who the fuck knows? You've spent significant time with Clay lately, what does your gut tell you?"

"That Clay is clueless. He seems to regret what happened to Caterina. Joanna certainly believes that. She has them over at our farm often because she wants them to have a safe space to get to know each other. If I find out Clay has blood on his hands, and I let him have access to Joanna—"

"I'll be right there with you. None of us knew Clay before his best friend married my sister. He's been considered one of us since then. I should have looked into his history more."

"There was a lot going on. I didn't do the kind of background check on him I normally would have."

"Clay's a tough one. His version of the truth has always been—flexible."

"It's difficult to believe Clay has no idea what happened to his uncle."

"But not impossible. Dammit, I was beginning to like the guy."

"Me too. He can be a bit much in large doses, but I appreciate what he's done with his Gold Star initiative. I'd be able to tolerate him more if he wasn't so . . ."

"Fairy Godfather-ish?"

"Yes." Bradford sighed and flexed his hands on his steering wheel. "Joanna says we all deal with trauma in our own way. I tend to want to punch everyone in the face, Clay prances around tossing financially irresponsible pixie dust on everyone."

"That's an accurate description of both of you." After a pause, Ian asked, "How did Cooper stay hidden for so long?"

"There's no trace of Cooper Davis or Landon online after he was withdrawn from school. Not a single post by him or about him on social media accounts. Nothing. No credit card charges made, no bank accounts opened, not even a cell phone in the name of either. He went completely off the grid."

"He knows something."

"Absolutely. As do the people who normally would be looking for him."

"This is more complicated than anticipated. I should fly up."

"No need. All I'm doing is gathering information at this point."

"Okay, but if you learn anything new—"

"You'll be the second to know."

"How much did you tell Joanna?"

"Everything. She and I don't have secrets from each other."

"That's beautiful," Ian mocked.

Bradford retorted, "Like you're not the fucking same way with Claire."

Rather than acknowledging what they both knew to be true, Ian ended the call with a chuckle and a request for daily updates.

Chapter Nineteen

Amanda

I TOOK A little extra time on my appearance as I got ready for Mel and Mike's bonfire. When Cooper had dropped me off that morning, he'd first asked if I was planning to go and then if I wanted him to take me.

Um, hell yes?

Was this officially our first date? It certainly felt like it. I didn't want to put too much importance on it because there was still so much we needed to work through, but I couldn't not be excited.

My father smiled when I walked down the stairs. "You're glowing."

I blushed and made a face. "Am I that obvious?"

My mother walked out of the living room and added, "I'd tell you to be careful, but you're old enough to make your own decisions." She looked at my empty hands. "What dish are you taking?"

"Oh, shit." With everything that was going on, I totally forgot.

"Stop by Manju's. She'll have something ready to go.

She's always prepared. And she drops fresh donuts right around this time."

"Good idea." Manju's Donuts was a misnomer since they also served sandwiches and a variety of other desserts. Manju and her husband had come to Driverton straight from Nepal, seeking a fresh start. Raised in a city as the only daughter of a wealthy family, her future had seemed predetermined. Arranged marriages were the expectation and she'd believed that was her destiny—then she met Adarsh.

He was an orphan from a remote mountain town who had come to the city to work. They met by chance when she'd accidentally left her phone on a stone bench in a park, and he'd found it. Seeking the owner, he'd called one of the numbers and Manju had gone with a female friend to retrieve her phone. All it had taken was that one meeting for the two to know they were meant to be together.

Manju said her normally supportive parents had done everything short of locking her in the house to keep her from him. In the end, embarrassed and angry, her parents had given her an ultimatum of Adarsh or them. She'd chosen him and ran away to the United States to marry him.

What brought them to Driverton was still a mystery, but their choice of occupation wasn't. The story was that Ollie's father befriended them and convinced them that every town, even one as small as ours, needed a donut shop. When Adarsh and Manju had been declined a loan from the bank, Ollie's father had organized a fundraiser for them and had raised just enough to rent the building they later purchased, and Manju's Donuts was born. Thirty years later they had two children in college, a son in New York, and a daughter in Boston, both studying medicine and a strong track record for doing fundraisers for any family in town with a need. Their menu was top notch, but they could have served shit on a shingle, and we would have continued to patronize them because they were one of us.

"Are you going to the bonfire with Cooper?" my father asked.

"Yes." I waited a beat for a hint of his feelings on that.

"Good," was all he said.

I grimaced. My father hadn't said much after learning more about Cooper's history, but I could see that he was now more cautious with him . . . at least where I was concerned.

My mother tucked one of my wayward curls behind my ear. "Try not to have sex with him for a couple of days."

I gasped. "Mom."

She waved a hand in the air. "I'm just suggesting you tap the brakes a little while things are so complicated."

My father groaned.

That didn't stop my mother. "You can say it's none of our business, but I don't want to see you hurt. This is a tough time for Cooper. Heating things up between the two of you right now might be too much for him."

My father cut in with, "It's time for him to step up or step off. I understand he went through something awful, but if he wants to keep my respect—"

"Dad," I cut in. "I love you, but this isn't about you." I took one of my mother's hands in mine. "I love you too,

Mom, and I hear you, but I need to follow my heart on this one. Cooper needs me in his corner right now. He needs all of us." I turned to meet my father's gaze. "I'm guessing that in the beginning people advised Mom to be careful around you. They might have even told you to stay away from her. Aren't you glad neither of you listened?"

My father moved closer to my mother, put his arm around her, and kissed her temple. "How annoying is it that our daughter is not only lecturing us now, but she's also frequently right?"

My mother rested her head on my father's shoulder. "It's rough. I'm also so excited about having a grandchild that I can't even be disappointed she doesn't know the importance of condoms."

"Mom." I said her name in reprimand again. "What happened to your filter?" My mother had never been quite so outspoken.

"The chemo killed it along with my cancer," she said with a straight face, then smiled.

Oh, boy. I chuckled and shook my head as I imagined where this trend may take both of my parents as they aged. Whatever I'd been about to say was lost when Cooper knocked on the screen door before opening it.

"Pete." He said my father's name in greeting then turned to my mother. "Dotty, you look like you're feeling better every day."

She gave him a warm hug, an act that seemed to surprise only me. "So do you."

"I am." He ducked his head as he stepped back and

smiled before addressing me. "You ready?"

The part of me that had hoped for a compliment from him was more than satisfied by the way the air sizzled and desire darkened his eyes as he looked me over. Words were not necessary when a man looked at a woman the way he was looking at me.

My father cleared his throat. "We were just suggesting you and Amanda stop by Manju's."

Cooper's face reddened as if he'd forgotten we weren't alone. "Then we should get going because it closes early the night of a bonfire, something about Manju and Adarsh not wanting to miss it."

I gave both of my parents a quick kiss on the cheek and went to stand near Cooper. It would have been so natural to slip my hand into his, but we weren't quite there yet.

"We're not going to this one," my father said. "Your mother and I thought we'd have a nice quiet night alone."

"So, see you both tomorrow," my mother said cheekily. "No need to text us unless you're *coming home*. We only want to know if we need to contain ourselves to our bedroom." She winked.

Cooper coughed.

"Mom." I covered my face with one hand then hastily. This time I did grab Cooper's hand but just to drag him out of my house. Only once we were inside his truck did I say, "I'm sorry about that."

His smile eased my embarrassment. "Come here."

He didn't have to say that twice. I scooted closer.

His hands dug into my hair and he claimed my mouth

with the hunger of a lover returning from war. An equal need rose in me. Had it really only been a few hours? That's not how it felt.

There are kisses that rev a person's engine and there are others that touch a person's heart. This one seared me straight to my soul. No one could have convinced me that we weren't two halves of a whole.

When he raised his head, we were both breathing so raggedly it was comical in the quiet of the truck. "Where are we going?" he asked in a husky voice.

"Manju's?" I was tempted to suggest we skip the bonfire, but these bonfires were important to Mike and Mel as well as to the town. I wanted to be part of that. I wanted *us* to be.

He kissed me again and murmured. "It's so close to my place we could walk over."

Oh, yes. "We should buy the food first." I arched my back as he began to trail kisses down my neck.

"No one would care if we're late to the bonfire."

"Better than being early." I glanced back at the house and saw that my parents had closed the door. "We should probably continue this elsewhere."

He straightened, shook his head, and started the engine of his truck. "I blame you for looking so damn hot."

That brought a huge smile to my face. "Guilty and shamelessly so."

Chapter Twenty

Cooper

THE SUN WAS just beginning to set when I accepted a beer from Everette in Mike and Mel's backyard. No one mentioned our late arrival, not even Manju who'd reopened because Amanda and I hadn't made it to her shop before stopping at my place.

That Manju was still in her shop meant she'd likely been asked to linger. She and Dotty were close, so it was a safe bet that a phone call had been made.

I hadn't felt guilty at all.

Priorities.

Amanda and I had walked into the party together, hand in hand. I'd never allowed myself to be part of a couple and I expected it to be more awkward than it was. We had received a few odd looks, but not the openly curious type Levi had given us in the alley.

They knew.

But how much?

Soon after we'd arrived, Mel and Mike had come over to greet us. Although Amanda had been born and raised in

Driverton, she'd spent enough time away that their conversation was still about reconnecting. These people genuinely cared about Amanda, and she returned that feeling. It was a bond I wanted to encourage so I didn't remain at her side. As soon as Amanda was relaxed and laughing, I walked away. Their conversation continued, more people joined them and the joy on her face made it impossible for me to look away from her.

Watching her filled me with a feeling akin to the pleasure found in plopping onto a soft couch at the end of a long day or the first bite of something after going too long without food. I was familiar with lonely, angry, scared, and numb . . . was this what *happy* felt like?

That's my woman.

She's having my baby.

"I don't have to ask you how things are going. Your smile says it all," Everette said. Only then did I realize I'd yet to thank him for the drink.

"Thanks."

"It's good to have you back." Everette was a gentle giant who could have played professional football if he cared about sports at all. He lived with his parents and made his living selling large wood sculptures he created with a chainsaw. They sold well, but no one would have guessed that by looking at him. He put most of his earnings toward paying for his younger siblings to go to college. If there'd ever been a time when I'd asked him for help and he'd refused, I couldn't remember it. Even by Driverton's standards, he was exceptionally good-hearted.

I took a swig of the beer. "It's good to be back."

After a moment, he said, "So, you're rich, huh?"

I tensed. I'd let how good being with Amanda felt take my focus from what needed to be addressed before we could really be together. Tom had said he would talk to Everette because his cousin was in the FBI. "I was born with money, but that's not my current financial situation."

"I spoke to Simon. He was fascinated by the idea that so much of what happened to you wasn't public."

I held back my initial sarcastic retort. Everette was trying to help. "How much did you tell him?"

"He needed to know everything. Don't worry, he's good at what he does. He promised that if he comes across anything incriminating, he'll wipe it if that's at all possible."

My throat tightened, but I had to ask, "About my uncle as well as what happened after that?"

Everette nodded slowly. "He agreed with Tom that neither was a crime."

I sighed. "Nice as that is to hear, tell him not to get involved."

"Too late, he already knows all about what you and Tom have been doing on the side. In his mind you're a fucking hero and helping you is a public service." After a pause, Everette added, "I had a general idea of what you were doing when you left town, but when Simon and Tom discussed it and I heard the details . . . I have to say if you ever need backup for one of those jobs you can call me."

I took another swig of beer before answering. "A lot of what we've done steps outside what would be considered legal, and you've seen the condition I often return in. We do whatever is necessary to get those kids home. It's not a job for someone who has responsibilities or anything to lose."

"So, you're leaving that behind?" He nodded toward Amanda. "Now that you have both."

My head snapped back. I hadn't thought that far ahead. "I don't know."

"That would be a shame because from what I heard you were making a huge difference."

I ran a hand through my hair. It was difficult to worry about the safety of abstract children when my own child might be in imminent danger. "It would be." My gaze returned to Amanda. "I have some things to sort through though before I can consider taking on another job."

"Your brother."

"Yes." I bit out the word.

"Simon told us what to watch for."

"And that is?"

"Anyone unusual. Anyone asking questions about you. He warned us that our technology can be used as surveillance devices. Scary shit."

"When you say *us* . . ."

"Simon gathered a few of us: me, Levi, Ollie, Mike because we're your friends." That wasn't good. Everette continued, "Adarsh and Manju because a stranger would seek out their shop for coffee. Robbie because he took over the gas station for his father and everyone stops there."

"So, is there anyone in town who doesn't know my business?"

"By now?" Everette scratched his chin. "Doubt it."

"Perfect," I said with some sarcasm.

"The good news is that they're all on your side. Although Mrs. Williams says if you don't marry Amanda she'll find her some husband material. She's started a list of who is both straight and single within a sixty-mile radius, so the clock is ticking on that front."

I laughed even though I didn't find it all that funny and shook my head. I still hadn't allowed myself to believe Amanda and I would make it as far as marriage. There were so many hurdles between where we were and that. "I'll keep that in mind."

"My name is probably on that list."

Now he had my attention and not in a good way. I said everything I had to with one look.

He smiled. "I've never seen you territorial about anyone."

I gave him another long look.

He looked away, took another swig of his beer then said, "I'm happy for you."

I relaxed.

A short silence followed during which I finished my beer as Everette did the same. "Cooper."

"Yeah?"

"What you went through—"

"I'd rather not talk about it."

"Because it hurts too much to remember?"

My hand clenched on the beer can so tightly I crushed it. "Because there's nothing about myself from back then that

I'm proud of."

Everette crushed his own can in his hand. "I feel that about who I am today."

I glanced at him in surprise.

He continued, "You're off saving lives and starting a family. Where will I be in five years? Ten? Still living with my parents? I never went to college. The only thing I know how to do is make chainsaw sculptures and what the hell kind of skill is that? I'm not even the person people call when they need shit fixed."

"Were you doing shots with Levi before I got here?"

"A ton of the Jell-O ones." He made a face then swayed. "At my size do you know how many it takes to have any effect at all?"

"No, but it looks like you've discovered your limit. I'd stop there."

He nodded. "I am pretty buzzed."

"You shouldn't drive anywhere."

"Ollie said he'd drive, but he and Levi were downing the shots right along with me, so I don't know how that's going to work out."

"I have my truck. You guys can ride home in the flatbed of it."

"I don't care if you did kill two people, you're a good friend, Cooper."

"Those two are just the ones I talk about." I don't know why I chose to flex my humor with a drunk Everette.

His eyes rounded. "No shit. How many?"

I cocked my head to the side. "Everette, you've known

me for a long time. You can't tell when I'm pulling your leg?"

"I believed you." He shook his head in sloppy wonder. "But you were just fucking with me?" He started laughing.

I smiled.

He laughed harder.

Across the lawn, Amanda turned and met my gaze. I mouthed, "I told you I'm funny."

Her face lit with a smile. Mel said something to her that drew Amanda's attention from me back to the conversation around her. I marveled at how lighthearted I felt. My brother might still be an issue, I could still end up with legal troubles, but I didn't want to think about any of that right then.

"Cooper," Everette said in a suddenly serious tone, "no one will hurt Amanda. We've got your back."

Without looking away from Amanda, I said, "I know. I'm damned lucky to have all of you in my life. You have a lot to be proud of, Everette, and when you're sober, I'll help you see that. If you want, I'll even teach you to fix shit so people can call you too."

Everette's response was a long, almost musical belch so close I could smell it. I looked from Amanda, to him, and back, then laughed.

This is my life.
And I don't hate it.
I don't hate it at all.

Chapter Twenty-One

Amanda

"S OME THINGS DON'T change. Guaranteed Everette and some of the others will end up in the back of Cooper's pickup. Every few months Cooper plays taxi service and we're grateful for it, but we need some new women to move to this town because without them those boys will never grow up," Mel said from beside me, pulling my attention from where Cooper was entertaining a sloshed Everette.

"Let me guess, Levi made moonshine Jell-O shots again?"

Mel laughed. "Like I said, not too much has changed." She glanced over at her husband. "Except Mike and I are considering trying for a fourth."

"That's awesome," I said with genuine enthusiasm.

"It's either proof that I've grown up or lost my mind." When she turned back to me, she was smiling.

Mike moved closer, put an arm around her and nuzzled her neck. "You're certifiable, but so am I, so it works."

I loved seeing them together. In high school they'd seemed interested in each other, but had always dated other people. Some things took time, I guess. *Like Cooper and me.*

I looked around the party and breathed it in. When I'd first returned home, I'd felt like an outsider, but the more time I was back the more I wondered how I'd ever thought there was a better place. "Mike, I love that you do these bonfires and that everyone comes. I was sad when I heard your parents were giving up the tradition. I should have known you'd continue it."

"There was a while when we almost gave it up. When we had our oldest and were figuring out the whole parenting thing," Mike said.

Mel laughed at her husband. "Oh, yes. Remember how perfect we thought everything had to be?" Then she looked at me. "I'd tell you to not obsess, but you will. It's natural. For our first one if a binkie fell to the floor, we boiled it to get it sterile again. Our second one I used soap and water from the sink. Now I wipe it off on my jeans or pop it in my own mouth for a second."

As soon as Cooper had walked away, Mel had told me she'd heard I was pregnant and offered support. Manju had come over to express the same sentiment. Mrs. Williams had grilled me on how serious I felt Cooper was taking the responsibility of becoming a father. There was a time when I would have felt their questions were intrusive, but I'd experienced the opposite and liked it less. The people in Driverton didn't maintain the same boundaries as my friends in the city had, and that explained why I'd felt lonely even when I wasn't alone there.

When Mrs. Williams interrogated me, it was because she cared. Mel wanted to be on the list of people I called with questions for the same reason. Manju was missing her children and would spoil me with treats and attention if I let her. "It's really good to be back," I said in a gush.

Mel hugged Mike. "We've missed you."

"I don't regret leaving because I learned a lot about myself, but this is my home."

"Speaking of home," Manju cut in. "Your parents aren't coming tonight?"

I rolled my eyes skyward and smiled. "They wanted some private time."

A general laugh rolled through the group. Mike joked, "Having you back in the house must be rough on them."

Smiling, Mel added, "That answers the question if she's feeling better."

Manju added, "It's good to see your father smiling again as well. He didn't complain, but the last few months have been hard on him."

"I didn't know," I said softly. "But that's what brought me back."

Mrs. Williams scoffed at that. "Your decision had nothing to do with a certain man who can't take his eyes off you?"

In the city I might have chosen my response more carefully, but Mrs. Williams had changed my diaper more than once. "I've always had feelings for him, but we have things we need to work out before we can move forward."

"You won't be single long either way," Mrs. Williams said with confidence. "Between my sisters and me, we've come up with at least eleven single men in the area. I know you'll want to stay close to your parents so I'm crossing off any that might be unwilling to move to Driverton."

I laughed because she had to be kidding, then stopped abruptly when I realized she wasn't. "If things don't work out with Cooper, I won't be looking for a man any time soon."

Mrs. Williams leaned closer and said, "I'm saying you have options. Cooper is a good man, but don't settle for scraps if someone else would cater a whole meal for you."

I blinked a few times quickly. On one hand I was perfectly capable of raising a child on my own and the idea that I needed a man seemed outdated. On the other hand, the idea that Mrs. Williams and her sisters were out there interviewing prospective men for me was so sweet I leaned over and hugged her. "Thank you. I'll keep that in mind."

She was beaming when I stepped back. I glanced over at Cooper and was surprised to see him frowning. *I hope everything is okay over there.*

Mel interrupted that train of thought by saying, "What you should do, Mrs. Williams, is start of list of single women willing to move here. We've got some good men right here in town who could benefit from those matchmaking skills."

Mrs. Williams blushed. "I'm no matchmaker. It's just that I hate sitting back and watching this unfold and feeling powerless to help."

Aww, how could I not hug her again? I did. When I stepped back, I was wiping at my eyes. "How about if I come over this week and we play a few hands of spades? That would help me."

"I'd love that," Mrs. Williams said with another huge smile before glancing in Cooper's direction. "Your man is heading over here with a speed that suggests Everette told him I'm lining up marriage options for you. Good."

I turned and confirmed Cooper was striding over with an expression I couldn't decipher. He came to a stop right next to me and put an arm around my waist then gave my cheek a kiss in a deliciously possessive way that sent waves of warmth shooting through me. "Having a good time?" he asked in a deep voice.

"I am." I smiled cheerfully. "It's nice to catch up with everyone."

"Um-hmm," he said, then looked at Mrs. Williams. He brought two fingers to his eyes, then wagged them at her before pointing them back at his own eyes again, messaging that he was watching her.

Mrs. Williams cackled in response. "I regret nothing."

This time he smiled as well. "All I'm asking for is a moment to figure things out."

Hand on hip, Mrs. Williams leaned in. "Honey, you've had a decade. A lot of men wouldn't need more than a few minutes to determine Amanda is a catch."

Cooper's arm tightened on my waist and some of his humor left him. "How amazing Amanda is or isn't has never been in question." Mel, Mike, and Manju quickly excused themselves from the conversation.

Mrs. Williams didn't back down. "If you intend to use your past as an excuse to behave badly now, you'll find I have no patience with that."

Cooper straightened to his full height. "If it were my choice, no one in town would know anything about what happened before I came here. I don't use my past as an excuse for anything."

"No?" Mrs. Williams looked unimpressed, and I took a moment to marvel at the interaction between them. Cooper was hurt by her criticism but there was a beauty to that. He cared what she thought. And she was calling him out because to her he wasn't an outsider. "Amanda just asked if I'd like to play spades with her. I'd love to. You should come with her because that's what a man does when he makes a baby with someone. He sticks around for all the little moments in life that turn out being more important than whatever big issues he might think more pressing."

I looked from her face to Cooper's and back. "You're right," he said in a husky voice.

Her expression gentled. "Life is full of things to celebrate and things to mourn, Cooper. We decide what to fear and what to embrace. Katie told me you're afraid who will come here. Don't let the shadows convince you there is no sunlight. I have a shotgun and a shovel. Someone comes for you or Amanda, I'll greet them from my porch with a wave and a warning shot. All you need to worry about is that woman on your arm and that sweet child you're going to raise together."

Cooper shuddered against me and in a thick voice said, "Mrs. Williams, I can't marry Amanda . . ." I tensed and felt my world crashing in until he added, "because I just fell in love with you."

Mrs. Williams cackled again and swatted at him. "Oh,

you."

I let out a relieved laugh. "Well, I suppose I'll need that list after all."

"No," Cooper and Mrs. Williams said in unison.

Mrs. Williams added, "I'll hold onto it a little bit longer."

"I appreciate that," Cooper added, his smile returning.

After Mrs. Williams walked away, I turned and tipped my head back so I could meet Cooper's gaze. "Are you genuinely worried about me hearing about other single men?"

He hugged me to his chest. "I know you deserve better than I'm giving you. I wish it were as easy as choosing to not let my past affect me. Before coming here, Amanda, I lost everyone I've ever cared about. That's not an excuse, but it has framed my expectations for my life. I'm trying to change that. I thought confronting my brother would finally free me. I'm not so sure anymore. If I discover he played a role in what happened to my parents and my siblings, if I embrace the rage that will follow, I might do something that could cost me a future with you. I don't want that."

I held him as tightly as he was holding me. I couldn't imagine what I'd do if anyone intentionally hurt my parents or if everyone I loved started disappearing. I doubted I would have handled it as well as he had. "It's okay to not have all the answers, Cooper. I know I don't. What matters to me is that we try to find them together." He kissed me then and it was so sweet I nearly burst into tears.

When he raised his head, he said, "Amanda Glenford,

will you be my partner in crime? My ride or die? With a strong hope that we both come out of this alive?"

I searched his face. "That depends."

Concern filled his eyes. "On?"

"Would I have to share you with Mrs. Williams? I'm the jealous type."

He barked out a laugh. "I'll break things off with her."

"Then I'm in."

He glanced over to where Levi and Ollie were mock sword fighting with toys Mel's children had left out. "Even if being with me means playing midnight chauffeur to that crew?"

"Just like we used to in high school. Do you remember the time Levi made pot brownies instead of Jell-O shots and got the whole football team stoned? We drove them home in shifts."

Cooper laughed. "Yes, we did. They got in so much trouble with their parents and the coach they haven't done that since."

"Just Jell-O shots."

"And not even that often. I know leaving was tough but staying wasn't much easier for some of them. When you've always been part of something it's harder to see the value of it . . . or the importance of the role you play in it."

I searched his face. "Did Everette say something?"

"He did. And it helped me put some things into perspective. I've never turned down a job Tom brought me, but it also never mattered to me if I came back alive. I can't imagine not helping to find a missing child, but I intend to seek out less dangerous methods. When I find some, I'm going to involve Everette. He drinks because that's all he has that makes him feel good. I'd like to help him find something more."

I'd thought there was no way I could love Cooper more than I did, but whenever he opened up to me like that, I handed over another piece of my heart. Someday, I hoped we would be in a place where I could tell him that. Instead, I cleared my throat and said, "I'm not in the mood to text my parents, so it looks like I'm all yours tonight."

The heated look he gave me said it all.

My place was at his side, in his truck, in his bed. I was his.

And he was mine.

The rest? It didn't scare me.

Not anymore.

Chapter Twenty-Two

Bradford

A SMART MAN doesn't rush in without doing some reconnaissance first. Bradford spent a couple days in the towns surrounding Driverton, asking questions about it. What he learned shaped his approach.

Driverton had an extremely small population, wasn't known for being friendly to outsiders passing through, but tended to welcome those looking to move to the area. Bradford honed his story on the residents of the neighboring towns until he came up with one that seemed to warm the locals. Not an easy feat for a severely scarred man who looked like he'd lost a fight with a pit bull.

His childhood had not been an easy one. Raised in a foster home, he'd tried to pry his sister away from the gang she thought could replace the family they'd lost. Things had not gone well for his sister. Bradford had been too young to save her, but that hadn't stopped him from trying. Both his facial scars as well as those hidden beneath his clothing prevented him from being considered handsome, but to him they were badges of honor. Trying to extricate his sister from the gang had first gotten him beaten within an inch of dying then shot. He'd been in the hospital still recovering from that gunshot wound when his sister died from an overdose.

If it hadn't been for Alan, Bradford's foster father, Bradford would either be in prison or dead. He'd encouraged him to take his rage and enlist in the Army. "Want to fight? Fight for your country. Want to die? Die saving someone."

Funny how simple decisions could change the entire course of a person's life. The Army taught Bradford how to focus his rage for the benefit of humanity. Meeting Ian Barrington taught Bradford that his particularly deadly skillset could be highly lucrative. Falling in love with Joanna and marrying her pulled Bradford back from the brink of becoming like the monsters he helped remove from the earth.

Over the past few years, he'd found the value of a soft voice and a kind hand. He'd witnessed the healing power of love and a wholesome side of humanity he'd begun to doubt existed.

For the first time in Bradford's life, he had a large group of people he considered family. His in-laws, the Barringtons, the meatheads . . . Clay and his sister were an extension of that group. Those connections were why Bradford could now look himself in the mirror. They were his reason to get up every morning.

Vengeance had once been all that motivated him.

Since Joanna, he'd discovered . . . compassion? Whatever it was, it had him studying situations more carefully before acting. There were good people in the world and when he came across them, they inspired him to do more than battle evil.

Learning how to rehabilitate rescue horses had shown Bradford that trust can return. Kindness and patience matter. He'd once seen himself as a dark shadow of the man he might have been. Damaged. Worthless.

It's easy to be a hero when you have nothing to lose.

He thought about Cooper and how similar their lives had been despite coming from financial polar opposite families. A man didn't hide for as long as Cooper had unless he was either guilty, afraid, or both.

There was a time when Bradford would have automatically assumed the worst about both Cooper and Clay. Instead, he was striving to stay open-minded.

When Bradford pulled into a gas station on the edge of Driverton, he purposefully hunched his shoulders a little and forced a smile to his lips when he walked inside to pay. "Mind if I ask you a question?" he asked the young man behind the cash register.

The man's eyes widened then narrowed. "Sure."

"My wife and I are thinking about moving to this area. She runs a mini-horse rescue and we're looking for more land than we can afford in Rhode Island."

The young man looked Bradford over from head to toe. "That's what brought you to Driverton?"

With a self-deprecating laugh, Bradford said, "Actually, getting lost brought me to the area, but I did hear that there was a house for sale that might have several acres attached to it. I thought I should at least check it out."

"The Stanley house? It's been empty for a while, but the bones of it are solid."

"I'm not afraid of hard work. You ever try to trim a timid mini's hoof? Now that's a challenge."

The cashier relaxed a little. "I can imagine. My parents had a mini horse when I was little. His name was Sugar. Nothing sweet about him though."

Bradford chuckled. "My wife is good with them. She can bring a lamb out in any lion."

The cashier nodded. "My mom was the only one Sugar liked."

After glancing around, Bradford asked, "Is there a motel or bed-and-breakfast where I could snag a room from for the night? I was hoping to get to see that house and look around a bit before heading back."

"We don't get visitors around here. Mrs. Williams has an in-law apartment she lets former locals use who want to visit without staying with their parents. She won't take money, but if you see anything broken and fix it while you're there she appreciates it."

"How would I contact her?"

He typed a message on his phone, then gave Bradford the address. "She says you're welcome to it, but she wants to see a photo of your wife and her rescue."

"I look forward to showing her both."

"She also said her washer just started making a gurgling sound."

"I don't know much about washing machines."

"Probably something clogging the drain line. What you'll

need for that is a snake cable. I've got one I can lend you. Pull the washer from the wall, unplug it, disconnect the hose then snake the pipe. It's usually that easy."

"Sounds doable. I'll google it to make sure, but yeah, I'll borrow the snake cable. Want me to leave any kind of collateral?"

"No. Mrs. Williams will make sure I get it back. We watch out for each other in this town."

Bradford nodded and smiled, careful to not give away that he'd heard the warning in Robbie's tone. "So, it'd be a good place to raise children."

More of the cashier's guard lowered. "I intend to bring mine up here."

He looked young to have children and there was no ring on his finger. Bradford didn't care about either. His only goal was to get the cashier to open up to him. "How many do you have?"

"None." The man shrugged. "Not a wife either, but I have a girlfriend who gets along with my parents and that's a start."

His sincerity amused Bradford, but he kept that from his expression. "Sure is. I'm tight with my wife's family. Sadly, I have no one on my side."

"Sorry to hear that." The man nodded toward a carafe of coffee. "Pour yourself a cup. No charge."

"Thanks," Bradford turned to do that. "Warm and welcoming. This is exactly the kind of town my wife and I are looking for. My name is Bradford."

That brought a smile to the man's face. "Robbie."

Bradford poured himself a coffee and referenced the glass covered pastries on one end of the counter. "My wife loves pastries. I'll have to stock up before I leave."

"You can pick up more at Manju's Donuts. It's on Main Street. And it's cheaper there. I upcharge here for the convenience."

"Good to know."

Robbie walked away then returned with a box of tools and cable. He placed it beside the cash register. "If you see anything else at Mrs. Williams's house that needs a quick fix, don't be shy. If you're even thinking about moving here you'll want to be on her good side. She can patch you up faster than any paramedic and if your wife goes into labor in a snowstorm, she's delivered more than one baby. Just watch your language around her. She would switch a preacher if he used the Lord's name in vain around her. She doesn't play."

Impressive. Bradford was actually looking forward to meeting her after that kind of intro. "Thanks for the heads-up. I have more than my fair share of scars already." Part of getting a person to lower their guard was to acknowledge the things that might give them concern. Bradford was well aware how his appearance affected people's perception of him.

Robbie looked him over without asking the questions that showed in his eyes. Bradford knew he'd have to address them to increase Robbie's ease around him.

He touched one of the scars on his cheek. "Tough childhood. I'm looking for better for my family."

"You couldn't get better than Driverton," Robbie said. "Not too much happens here but that's the way we like it.

Everyone knows everyone else's business. This is the wrong town for you if you've got secrets you want to keep."

Bradford's eyebrows rose. Had he underestimated Robbie? There was no reason anyone should suspect his purpose for being in Driverton, but Bradford's instincts told him there was more going on than he was aware of.

A town without its own police force . . . could there be a criminal element that the surrounding population wasn't aware of? He hoped not. A part of him needed to believe that small towns were as wholesome as the fresh baked goods he found himself reaching for. He bought a few items for himself and a box for Mrs. Williams. After paying, Bradford asked, "Is there a local restaurant or pub you suggest? After I settle in, I'm sure I'll be hunting down a beer and a meal."

"Little Willie's Pub is the only action in town. Ollie is the owner's name. Tell him I sent you and you might get a free appetizer."

"That's really kind of you. Thank you."

"Oh, and don't flirt with the waitresses. That never turns out well."

"Happily married."

Robbie nodded. "Nice to meet you, Bradford. Say hi to Mrs. Williams for me."

"I will."

Despite not having asked a single question about Cooper, Bradford was pleased with the groundwork he was laying for the people in town. If Driverton was anything like it presented itself initially, Bradford could completely understand why Cooper had stayed.

But what brought him here?

Chapter Twenty-Three

Cooper

I WAS ON a ladder stocking a shelf in the hardware store when Amanda sprinted in, waving her phone at me. "Cooper," her voice was breathless and anxious. "I just received a text from the lab. My doctor's office has the results."

I hopped down from the ladder. "And?"

She hugged the phone to her chest. "I didn't want to call without you."

Her faith in me and what we had rocked me back onto my heels. I didn't deserve her, but I'd spend the rest of my life trying to. "Come here."

She walked right into my arms as if we'd been together forever then turned so her shoulder rested against my chest. "This is it," she said. "You either have the gene or you don't. If you don't, I have a regular pregnancy. If you do, I schedule treatments and start praying a whole lot more."

I kissed her temple. "It's going to be okay."

"I know," she said but didn't sound certain. "Growing up I heard stories of children in my family not making it past the first few months of life. It was always sad, but it didn't feel real because I didn't know them. There's a good prognosis with early treatment now, but I don't want the baby to have Festner's. I don't know if I can handle that."

"You *can*." Added to her mother's recent battle with cancer, I could imagine that worrying about her child's survival as well could be overwhelming. "*We* can. Call the doctor." My urgency to know mirrored hers.

With shaking hands, she did. When the other side answered, she said, "Hello, this is Amanda Glenford. I'm calling for the results of the genetic test we had done." Amanda put the call on speaker so I could hear as well.

"The doctor is with someone right now, but Mr. Landon signed the release form so I can give you that information or I can have the doctor call you when she's free."

"I need to know," Amanda said. "Did you find the gene?"

I held my breath and sent up a prayer of my own. With all the mistakes I'd made and all the challenges that loomed before us, one thing had to go right for us. Just one sign was all I needed.

"The lab reported no sign of the Festner's gene in the blood sample. There is no follow-up needed with your doctor outside of going ahead with a regular OB schedule."

"Are you sure?" Tears began flowing down Amanda's cheeks.

I let out a long, relieved breath.

"It's a routine test. We can put in for a retest, but I haven't personally seen different results come back."

"Thank you," Amanda said with a huge smile while wiping away her tears. "Thank you so much." She ended the call then turned and the smile she gave me echoed in my heart. "The baby is going to be fine."

I blinked a few times quickly as emotion welled within me. "I told you. You were worried about nothing."

She pushed at my chest playfully. "Just me?"

I wiped at the corners of my eyes. "Yep, I wasn't worried at all."

Amanda pocketed her phone and leaned back in my arms. "Is it crazy that I want to celebrate this? Call my father. See if you can close the store early. Let's go do something."

I kissed her briefly and murmured, "What would you like to do?"

Her expression turned hopeful. "Would you go with me to see the Stanley house? I didn't want to think about it seriously if I might need money for genetic therapy, but I'd like to evaluate how much work the inside of it would need and if it could be done before the baby arrives."

I hated that I couldn't tell her I'd buy it for her. My family's money had never been important to me, but I needed to provide for my woman and child. "It's been sitting empty for a while. There might be issues even in the plumbing that wouldn't be immediately obvious."

Her expression lost some of its glow. "Do you think the house isn't worth it?"

It wasn't, but I couldn't say that. With others I'd always been clear about how little of what they felt was my responsibility, but that wasn't how it was for me with Amanda. Her happiness was right up there in importance with her safety. I'd work every night and weekend on the house if that's what it took to have it ready for when the baby came. I might not be able to give her money for the down payment, but I could help her lower the price. "It's in rough shape, but we can head over there today and look around. The Stanley kids don't want it. They're holding on to it because they think it could be worth more in the future. That's not the case. Let's take some photos and show them why."

That returned the smile to her face. I called to ask Pete if he cared if we closed up early. Amanda chimed in with her news. He and Dotty were so happy I'm pretty sure I could have asked for anything and he would have agreed to it.

Her mother added, "The Stanley house could be beautiful again. If it's still there, there is a copper soaking tub that Richie's father bought his mother when he returned from World War II. She was a large woman, so he had it made extra wide and told her it was the norm. Sadly, that story has survived three generations, so she eventually figured it out."

Pete said, "She was a beautiful woman in all the photos I've seen of her, but I've never minded a little meat on a woman."

"And this is where your father stops talking before he ends up on the couch," Dotty interjected.

I exchanged a look with Amanda. She was as close to bursting out laughing as I was.

"I'll call you later to tell you what we think of the house," Amanda said quickly.

In the background of the call her father said, "Aww, Dotty, I wasn't referring to you. I meant extra weight on *other women*."

Amanda did laugh at that. "Dad, I love you, stop. That's worse."

I couldn't help but say, "Fall back, Pete. Only landmines lie ahead."

"And burnt dinners," Dotty added. There was too much laughter in her voice for anyone to be worried. She and Pete bickered, but I'd never seen them actually argue about anything of substance.

"I love you, Dotty," Pete said, followed by a loud smack of a kiss.

Chuckling, I ended the call. "Your parents crack me up."

Amanda wrapped her arms around my neck and smiled up at me. "And they adore you. I love that you're close."

Hugging her flush against me, I gave her a slow, long kiss before answering. "Well, they did make one of my favorite people."

"*One of them?*" she arched an eyebrow playfully. "As in there are others you feel the same way for?"

She was her mother in many ways and there was nothing I didn't love about that. Dotty was a beauty inside and out. "About that Stanley house. I don't believe we need to tell anyone we're heading over. They keep the key beneath the front mat even though I doubt the doors are locked."

Her expression turned more serious. "I love you, Cooper. I don't know if this is the right time to say it, but I can't hold it in anymore. I want to be with you. Not just today. Forever."

I cupped her face between my hands. "I love you too, Amanda. You have me believing that dreams actually can come true and that's scary as all hell. But I want to be with you too—and forever doesn't seem like long enough."

We kissed again with a passion that sent us back upstairs to my room before we went anywhere. Hours later, when we parked in front of the Stanley house, she placed her hand on my thigh and we exchanged a look filled with promises and hope.

That moment was so perfect I wished I could freeze time. I didn't want anything beyond this woman, this life, and the way I felt every time she looked at me.

A little voice in the back of my head said nothing that good could last, but I got out of the truck, rushed around to open Amanda's door, and pushed that fear back. So many things in my life had felt out of my control.

My family.

My guilt.

My loneliness.

My anger.

Was all of that truly a choice? If so . . .

I don't choose those anymore. I raised Amanda's hand to my lips and kissed the back of it. *I choose her and fatherhood.*

Everything else be damned.

Chapter Twenty-Four

Amanda

I *JUST TOLD Cooper I love him, and the sky didn't fall. He didn't sprint in the other direction or give a painful, I-wish-I-could-say-it-back-but-I-can't look.*

He said it.

He loves me.

Cooper wasn't one of those men who said things he didn't mean. He also didn't talk about his feelings easily. I wanted him to repeat those three beautiful words to me again and again, but once was magical enough.

I could have stood there all day staring up into his eyes, but I was excited about seeing the inside of the Stanley house. Evaluating it with Cooper meant even more now that it felt like living there together was something that would happen. "I've always wanted to see the inside of this house."

He frowned. "You've never gone in?"

"The Stanley's weren't all that friendly and I'd moved away by the time the house went on the market."

"Prepare yourself then. You might change your mind about wanting it once you experience it."

That was an odd way of describing touring the inside. "Now I'm scared."

He shot me a crooked smile. "There's nothing inside to fear unless you have a phobia of clutter, mold, and outdated furniture."

I took in the outside of the home. Set on a fifteen-acre plot, the two-story white house sprawled in both directions. The main part of the house was majestic with large windows and a beautiful sunroom that wrapped around a corner of it. The number of chimneys suggested numerous fireplaces. Mismatched additions, also painted white, had been built off the main house, giving the impression that three separate houses had been mashed together. "I know it's an odd house, but something about it has always called to me."

Cooper linked his hand with mine and led me up the stone steps, warning me to be careful of the loose stones, then onto a large porch that had also seen better days. Some of the floorboards were rotted and a few of the porch ceiling boards had separated and were hanging down.

This could be a real money pit.

As if hearing my thoughts, Cooper gave my hand a supportive squeeze. "Those are cosmetic issues. I can fix those."

I smiled, nodded, and followed him through the front door. No pregnant woman should inhale the smell that met me as we stepped inside. I turned and almost threw up on Cooper. He quickly took a step back. My stomach settled, but I had to ask, "Is there something dead in here?"

"No, I think that's lingering smell of animal waste. Mr. Stanley had a dog he stopped letting outside near the end of his life. We tried to help him, tried to get his family involved. Eventually Tom came with animal control, and they confiscated his dog. I adopted it so he could still see him. Mr. Stanley died a few months later and his dog soon afterward."

I swallowed hard. "Did he die here?" That might be a deal breaker for me.

"No, his kids put him in nursing care a few weeks before he passed. The town would have come and cleaned the house for them, but they were more angry than grateful for what we tried to do for Mr. Stanley. He was stubborn to the end. It wasn't easy to help him."

"The apple didn't fall far from the tree I guess." My nausea subsided so I took another step into the house. "Is the entire house carpeted?" Stained mauve carpet stretched out in every direction, ruining what otherwise could have been a beautiful entry.

"Yes, even the bathrooms."

"That's gross."

"Carpeting can be pulled up. If the wooden floors beneath are in salvageable condition his obsession with carpeting might even be a benefit. Depends on how much urine soaked through."

I slumped a little. "I'd be better off staying with my parents. This place is disgusting and there's no way it could be ready before the baby arrives."

He turned me toward him. "Hey, I'm the pessimistic one, remember? You're the one with the dreams and the fire to make them come true. There are parts of this house I like."

"Such as?"

"Come on." He gave my hand a little tug and led me to the sunroom and for just a moment I forgot to be disgusted by the rug beneath my feet. The windows provided a panoramic view of fields of tall grass then woods. On the left of the room an enormous fireplace took up most of the wall, large enough that someone could stand in it. "He told me once that this was his wife's favorite room."

"I can see why." Something occurred to me that had me asking, "Mr. Stanley talked to you? I thought he hated everyone."

"We weren't friends, but I brought him groceries and tools now and then. I understood him."

Shaking my head, I looked around at the stacks of junk that filled every corner. Mr. Stanley was one of the few in town who not too many people liked—mostly because he hadn't liked anyone in town. "What did you see that others didn't?"

"Mr. Stanley was never right after the war. I don't know what happened there, but he couldn't stand people or crowds afterward. He couldn't tolerate the sound of footsteps, so he carpeted his whole house. His children moved away. His wife died. All he had was this house and his dog." Cooper walked to a pile of newspapers and blew the dust off one that had yellowed with age.

I looked at the newspaper in his hand. "Are you sure you want to touch anything in here?"

"This looks like trash, doesn't it?" He turned the paper

so I could read the headline. It was an announcement of a holiday parade. I scanned the page.

"Yes?"

"It's actually a shrine to his wife. After she passed away, he collected anything and everything that reminded him of her and put it here in her favorite room. They went to that parade together before he was deployed. His children called him a hoarder and fought with him to empty the house. I came over to help him, but when he told me why he was collecting things I didn't have the heart to throw any of it away."

My chest tightened as I felt Cooper's pain. "I didn't know, Cooper. This isn't the right house for us."

The corners of his eyes crinkled. "Us. I like that."

I smiled and wrapped my arms around him. "I'm your ride or die. Did you think I wouldn't want you here with me?"

His eyes darkened. "You could choose a man from a normal family, one with less issues than I have." He swallowed visibly. "Why were you drawn to this house?"

Was he asking me if my love for him was born in pity? If so, he couldn't be more wrong. "It's strong, proud, and still standing even though it wasn't treasured the way it should have been." I raised a hand to cup one of his cheeks. "Like you."

"I'm all in, Amanda." He dropped the paper and wrapped his arms around me. "I want to believe I can make you happy, but look around. He loved his wife, and this is what he gave her."

I did look around—with kinder eyes than I had before. "A beautiful house, two children, and his love. My mother has been talking a lot about her mortality lately and at first it was scary to me. I mean, I know we all die, but I don't want to think about it. She's not afraid though, and that's changing how I think about my own mortality. It's not about how it ends—it's about all the moments, all the joy, we soak up as we go through it. That it isn't forever can be terrifying or it can be a reminder to grab life with both hands and live the way we want to—unafraid and free because it's all temporary. Mr. Stanley isn't here anymore. He's somewhere with his wife, probably walking on clouds so footsteps are no longer an issue. And, if the universe makes any sense at all, their dog is with them, pooping all over those clouds and it's no longer an issue."

Cooper chuckled and held me tighter. "That's an interesting image of heaven."

"Life is what we make it. Why wouldn't heaven be the same?"

He looked down at me with such love in his eyes I would have said that moment ranked as one of the most romantic in my life, except for the stench that made it impossible to truly bask in the glow of it. He asked, "Want to see the rest of the house?"

"I do."

As we walked out of the sunroom back into the hall, Cooper said, "Mr. Stanley also had a thing for urinals. They're in every bathroom."

"No."

"Yep. All five of them."

"Five bathrooms? How many bedrooms?"

"Five as well."

"Any rooms I shouldn't see? Cause I'm firmly on the fence about this house. I love the land. I can see the potential, but I don't know . . ."

"Don't go in the basement. It's damp and not well lit."

"So, maybe this isn't the house for us."

"There's one other room you should see."

We walked to a metal spiral staircase, and I paused. "Is it safe?"

"The frame of the house is solid."

"Okay." I headed up in front of him. "But I'm trusting you."

He gave my rump a light swat. "Get moving. It smells better up there."

When I reached the top of the stairs I gasped and looked around in wonder. The high ceiling allowed for tall walls of shelves all filled with books. It was dusty, but the woodwork was stunning. My mouth hung open as I made my way across the room to touch one of the rolling ladders. "It's like something out of a movie."

"This was another of her favorite rooms. He didn't leave the house, but he wanted to travel with her. He said they saw the world together through these books. I thought it was sad when he told me, but . . ."

"It's also kind of beautiful," I finished softly. "He obviously loved her very much." I touched the binding on one of the travel books. "I'm surprised their children didn't want any of this."

"The sale includes the contents of the house, so if you do buy the house, you'd score not only this library but all the carpeting as well."

I walked over to one of the windows and pulled back a musty drape, revealing a large stained-glass window. "What do you think, Cooper? Could you see us here?"

He stepped closer, wrapping his arms around me from behind. "I can see myself anywhere you are."

It felt like a dream and one I didn't want to wake from. I cuddled closer against his chest. "I want to stay in Driverton to be close to my parents." There was something else I felt needed to be said. "We could make this place ours and fill it with children."

He tensed behind me. *"Children?"*

"I had a great childhood, but I always wanted siblings. I wouldn't want to have just one child."

"You'd want to fill this house with them?"

I glanced back at him. "Too soon for that topic?"

He ran a hand through his hair. "I—I don't know." His expression was so concerned my heart ached for him. "Shouldn't we wait to see if I'm any good at parenting?"

I took his hand and laid it on my stomach. "Parenting is happening. What part do you think you won't be good at? Loving the child?"

"No," he said in a tone thick with emotion. "I already do."

"Sticking around?"

"I'm not going anywhere."

"Being kind to it? Listening when it needs you to? Being there for it when it's in pain? You're already proving with me that you can do all of that . . . and better than most. So, where would you fail?"

His face tightened and tears welled in his eyes. "I didn't save Caterina. I didn't save Collin. When the people I loved needed protection the most, I did nothing."

"What could you have done, Cooper? You were a child, and you didn't know what was true and what wasn't. If they were here today, they'd tell you the same thing I am. You didn't fail your family. Part of you knows that, but you still feel guilty that you survived and they didn't."

"Yes."

"I haven't experienced that kind of loss, but if something happened to me, I would want only the best for those I left behind. I don't believe your family is looking down on us wishing they were here instead of you. They loved you and they're proud that you're a survivor. If you'd gone instead of them isn't that how you'd feel?"

He sniffed and wiped a hand across his forehead. "It is."

"Then can you see why I'm not worried if you'll make a good parent? You are the most loyal, most loving person I've ever met. That's why you should change the first diaper."

A smile returned to his face. "Hold on, what?"

"Maybe all the diapers. You know, because you'll feel like you need to prove yourself and what better way than that?"

He laughed. "I see what you're doing here."

"Do you?" I fluttered my eyelashes at him.

"Taking advantage of a man at his lowest point," he

joked.

"How about we split diaper duty fifty/fifty?"

With a grin, he said, "I'll agree to that. Cooking too. Just because nothing you make tastes good doesn't mean we won't be taking turns."

My mouth rounded. "Rude," I said with a laugh.

He wiggled his eyebrows. "The truth hurts. Dotty is such a good cook, what happened to you?"

"Them's fighting words. I'll have you know I can cook a mean . . . Well, some people like my . . ." I stopped there when I couldn't think of a dish people had said they enjoyed. "I suppose you'll just have to give me lessons."

He nuzzled my neck. "I'd love to."

"And I'll teach you how to put the toilet seat down after each use."

He raised his head, laughter in his eyes, and said, "Are you suggesting we keep the urinals?"

"No," I said with such conviction I burst out laughing.

He joined in.

And I blurted out how I felt. "We could be happy here, Cooper."

His smile lit the room. "We already are."

Chapter Twenty-Five

Bradford

WHEN BRADFORD FIRST entered Little Willie's, he'd been offered a pretty standard menu and assessed the place as no different than any other watering hole he'd ever scoped out. When he told the waitress that Robbie had sent him the atmosphere changed. She called out a name across the pub, "Ollie, Robbie sent this guy over." And all eyes turned to Bradford's table.

A young man in his mid to late twenties came out from behind the bar. He was dressed casually, but considering the relaxed attire of the small number of other patrons it made sense. He ambled over. Bradford stood to shake his hand.

"Welcome to Driverton," Ollie said. "Robbie sent you?"

"He did," Bradford said, remaining standing. "My name is Bradford. I'm staying at Mrs. Williams's house tonight and checking out the area. My wife and I are considering moving up this way."

Ollie bent and said something to the waitress, then sat and waved for Bradford to sit as well. "We don't get a lot of people coming through here. You like game meat?"

Bradford sat, alert but not overly concerned. "Depends on how it's prepared."

Ollie's chest puffed. "I don't put it on the menu because it's just for the locals, but the recipes are as old as the town."

"Then I'd love to sample some."

"I thought you'd say that," Ollie said as the waitress returned with a variety of plated meats. "Tonight, we have venison sausage, quail nuggets, and beef jerky Everette's family donated to the pub."

"Donated?" Bradford picked up a slice of venison sausage and took a test bite. *Delicious.*

"I buy the alcohol and basics for the pub, but if people want to get fancy, they're welcome to bring their own."

It didn't sound like a solid business plan for a pub, but a bite of the jerky changed Bradford's opinion on whether outside foods could match those of a restaurant. It was just spicy enough with a satisfying texture. Bradford could have downed the plate. "I can see why you wouldn't turn this away."

"You open to meeting some of the locals?" Ollie asked.

He's doing my job for me. "Sure."

Ollie called two other men over. After they sat, Ollie said, "This is Everette."

"Bradford." Bradford said, "Your beef jerky is amazing."

Everette beamed. "Thanks."

Levi introduced himself then put a mason jar of dark liquid on the table. "You like moonshine, Bradford?"

"Not particularly." Especially not while working a case, which technically he was.

Levi raised the mason jar and gave it a shake. "Do you know how to tell the proof?"

"No idea," Bradford answered. His expertise was weaponry and hand-to-hand combat. Evaluating moonshine? He'd missed that day in covert operative school.

Ollie said, "The smaller and slower the bubbles disappear the lower the proof."

"It has something to do with alcohol being less dense than water. The atoms in alcohol are farther apart which means air bubbles are bigger and escape faster," Levi said.

"Look who's been googling moonshine," Everette joked.

"Knowledge is never a bad thing," Levi countered. "Just because your beef jerky has been the same for a hundred years doesn't mean I should quit striving to make the perfect drink."

"Hey, hey, hey," Ollie intervened, "I didn't bring you guys over to argue. Bradford is thinking about buying the old Stanley place. We should get to know him."

"You're right." Levi trotted off and returned a moment later with four shot glasses and shook the mason jar again. Large bubbles disappeared almost immediately. "Bradford, you have to try my home brew."

"I'll pass."

Levi filled all four shot glasses then placed them in front of the men. The others picked one of the glasses up. Levi said, "To friendship and loyalty."

How could Bradford not drink to that? He downed the shot then sucked in a harsh breath as it burned its way down his throat. It had been a while since he'd had more than beer, and moonshine had an almost instant kick to it.

Ollie refilled the glasses. "To towns so small maps forget to include them."

As they all raised their glasses, Bradford slowly picked up his again as well. The second shot went down smoother. The third even easier. Bradford's guard lowered as the rounds continued right through a game of darts. Then pool. Then darts again. More food was brought out.

Either Levi, Everette, and Ollie were the fucking funniest people on the planet, or Bradford was drunk for the first time in years. The trio took turns telling embarrassing stories about each other. When they asked him about his life, he found himself sharing more than he ever did. Nothing dark, but he talked about how his wife inspired him to be a better person and how he was finally in a good place in his life.

They'd all returned to the table for a round of burgers when an older man walked into the pub, stopped to talk to the waitress, then joined them. "I heard Robbie sent a friend over to meet Ollie."

Levi clapped Bradford on the back. "Bradford, meet Adarsh. His wife Manju makes the most incredible lemon squares."

Bradford rose to shake the man's hand. The room surprised him by spinning a little as he sat back down. "I bought a delicious-looking lemon square from the gas station. Were those hers?"

Adarsh smiled with pride. "Yes. My family runs Manju's Donuts. Robbie sees more out-of-towners than the Main Street does so he kindly allows us to sell them there as well."

He pulled a chair over from another table and joined them.

Bradford tried to remain focused and coherent. "Driverton is a tight-knit community." There was a slight slur to his words, but not enough to be noticeable—he hoped.

"Extremely," Adarsh added. "But also welcoming. My wife and I came here straight from Nepal. We thought it would be difficult to make friends, but the people here have become our American family."

It could have been the high-proof moonshine, but that was one of the most beautiful things Bradford had ever heard said about a town. Fabricating stories to get intel was part of his everyday job, but it felt out of place in Driverton. He forced himself to refocus on his purpose for being there. "Are there many transplants here?"

"Some," Adarsh said vaguely.

Bradford frowned. With how friendly everyone had been with him they should have been more open. He needed to put aside what he felt and spin whatever tale necessary to get the information he needed. This wasn't about making friends. "One of my old school buddies said he'd relocated in the area."

"Did he?" Adarsh said without asking more.

If the others at the table had heard the conversation, they didn't feel the need to contribute to it. Bradford added, "It's been a while since I've seen him. We weren't all that close I remember him saying he found a nice town he wanted to settle down in."

"What's his name?"

There was a sudden stillness to the group that had Bradford looking around. He didn't see anger or aggression in any of their eyes. "Cooper . . . Davis."

Adarsh shook his head. "Sorry. I don't know any Coopers."

"Or Davises," Everette added. "No Davis Coopers or Cooper Davises."

Odd.

"'Nother round?" Levi asked, turning Bradford's attention back to him.

"I shouldn't," Bradford said. *I'm going to feel this tomorrow.*

Adarsh said, "I think you've all had enough."

"Robbie sent him," Ollie said as if that was meaningful. "This is us helping."

Adarsh shook his head. "It wasn't necessary."

Helping? Bradford sat up straighter, swayed a little, then looked around the group again. *Are they deliberately getting me drunk?*

Everette stood. "That's a matter of op-onions." He laughed and corrected himself. "Opinions, not onions. Imagine if this was a matter that could only be handled with onions?"

Adarsh checked his phone and in an authoritative voice said, "Mrs. Williams's fridge stopped working again. There's one at the old police station that Tom donated for the break room. Are any of you sober enough to help me take it to her?"

"Sure," Ollie said. "Is it an emer-emergency? We were going to play another round of darts."

"She has medication that has to be refrigerated. If you're too drunk just tell me."

"Is there such a thing as too drunk?" Everette turned to Bradford. "How about you? You sober enough to help?"

"Absolutely," Bradford said out of pride rather than an actual assessment of his state.

"I'll drive," Adarsh said with a sigh. "Are you all coming?"

Nodding, Everette, Levi, and Ollie rose and began walking with Bradford and Adarsh toward the exit. "Bradford, all I have is my truck, but if you don't mind riding in the back with them, we can take one vehicle. None of you should be driving anyway."

After they sloppily made their way through the parking lot and rolled into the back of Adarsh's truck, Levi counted, "One. Two. Three. Four musketeers this time. If you move here, Bradford, we could make this a regular thing."

"He's not really moving here," Ollie said, then covered his mouth.

Everette swung a hand in the air. "Don't listen to them, Bradford. They don't make any damn sense when they drink. Never have. Levi's even worse when he's stoned. In high school he wanted to propose to Mary Singer. He smoked to work up his courage and ended up proposing to her mother."

Ollie burst out laughing. "Mr. Singer kicked Levi's ass. Was that why you gave up smoking, Levi?"

Levi shook his head. "No, it was that time we got the football team stoned and the whole town was grounded for a month." He frowned. "Mary never did forgive me. I saw her the last time she came home for a visit, and she wouldn't even look at me."

Bouncing around the flatbed of Adarsh's truck as it turned a corner, Bradford had to ask, "Were you sober?"

"Uh . . ."

Before Levi had a chance to answer, the truck pulled into a small parking lot of a building that was still labeled "Police." There was a light on inside. "I thought you said the building isn't being used anymore."

Adarsh answered from beside the truck. "It's not. Mrs. Williams said she'd meet us. She wants to make sure it's done right."

The door of the building opened. Mrs. Williams, cane in one hand, waved with her other for everyone to come. Bradford swayed as he made his way up the stairs but felt confident he could still be of use. Something wasn't right. He looked Mrs. Williams over as he walked through the door she held open. "You weren't using a cane earlier."

She smiled and shrugged. "I only need one when I'm tired. Thank you for coming to help, Bradford."

"You're welcome." Bradford pushed back the nagging feeling that he needed to be on guard with these people, but Mrs. Williams seemed as down to earth and harmless as anyone came.

She led the group through the front part of the station, past a few empty desks to a holding cell. She stepped inside. "This brings back memories," she said as she sat on the small bed, resting her cane against it. "I bet you won't believe it, but I used to raise my share of trouble when I was your age. I went through a pickpocketing stage. I thought it was hilarious. My parents didn't. I always returned what I took, but being able to swipe something off someone without them knowing—it was a rush." She gave the bed a pat. "My parents convinced Sheriff Liam, you all probably don't remember him, he died a good twenty years ago, but my parents asked him to help scare me straight. I spent a whole weekend in this cell after swiping a pen off Mr. O'Neil at church."

"At church?" Levi asked with a laugh. "You're headed to hell with the rest of us."

Mrs. Williams chuckled. "If so, I'll stoke the fire for you." She stood, looked around with a smile, then made her way out of the cell. "That was a long time ago, though. I'm sure I've been forgiven."

She stumbled, but Bradford caught her and helped her to a chair.

"Thank you," she said, then motioned toward the cell. "Do you mind getting me my cane, Bradford? I left it by the bed."

Without hesitation, Bradford walked into the cell to retrieve it. The sound of the door closing behind him didn't register as quickly as it would have had he been sober. He turned, cane in hand, in time to see Adarsh lock the door and step away.

"Did you get his gun?" Adarsh asked.

Mrs. Williams held it up then placed it on the desk beside her. "Of course. Did *you* get his cell phone, Levi?"

"His cell phone?" Levi's mouth dropped open. "Shit, I forgot."

"You had one job," Mrs. Williams said harshly.

"I did get him drunk," Levi said in defense.

"Levi," Mrs. Williams scolded. "I'm not your mother but someone needs to tell you it's time to grow up. Drunk isn't cute." She placed her hands on her hips. "And it's not helpful. With everything Cooper has done for you, you should have taken this more seriously." She frowned at Bradford. "Getting the phone now is going to be difficult."

"Try fucking impossible," Bradford growled. "And what happened to no one knowing a Cooper?"

"I'm sorry," Levi said, lowering his head.

Mrs. Williams's stance softened. "Don't be sorry, Levi, be better." She looked around at the three young men. "I made a list of eligible men for Amanda and I didn't put a single one of you on there and this is why."

"Not even me?" Everette asked.

Mrs. Williams shook her head. "I love all three of you like you were my own—"

"I *am* your own," Ollie said with a slur.

Mrs. Williams continued, "But none of you are living up to your potential. Ollie, Bradford fixed the washing machine I've been asking you to fix for weeks. Levi, if you spent half the time finding a market for your brews instead of drinking them, you'd be rich. And Everette . . ."

Despite the situation, Bradford found himself waiting to hear what she'd say to the third young man.

". . . you do so much for your family and that's a beautiful thing, but you need to do something for yourself as well. You're better than this."

"Yes, ma'am," Everette said in a humbled tone. "I know that."

She looked around. "You all are. So stop tearing each other down and encouraging each other to goof off. Lift each other up. Together, if you set your mind to it, you'd be unstoppable."

Ollie nodded. "I'll do better, Mom."

She sighed. "I don't want promises; I want action. Don't do better for me, do it for yourselves."

Levi sniffed. "Moonshine's illegal." He turned to Bradford. "I can't sell it, right?"

The whole situation felt surreal. Bradford's initial anger at being locked in a cell didn't feel as important as the scene unfolding before him. He walked over to the bars of the cell. "There are distilleries around the country that have started producing and selling high-proof alcohol they call moonshine. You couldn't legally sell what you make in your backyard, but I've heard many distilleries use old family moonshine recipes. One of them might be interested in buying yours or invest in the production process."

Mrs. Williams nodded in approval. "See, that's how you all need to start talking to each other." She stepped closer and looked Bradford over. "Now you. Do you have something you'd like to tell us?"

Bradford looked around at the group again. They were devious enough to have trapped him. What were their intentions? He'd dealt with double agents who were easier to read. "Me?"

"Who do you work for?" Mrs. Williams asked. "Who sent you?"

Why was it difficult to look her in the eye? "I don't know what you're talking about."

Her hands were back on her hips and Bradford felt as if he'd been called to the principal's office for misbehaving. "Did Clay Landon send you?"

"Yes," he admitted, just as surprised as they were at the confession.

"You go, Mrs. Williams," Everette said. "You're a fucking top-notch interrogator. Cracked him like a nut."

She turned to him. "Language."

He nodded. "Sorry."

Facing Bradford again, Mrs. Williams said, "Well, since you have your cell phone, you might as well call Mr. Landon and tell him if he wants our Cooper, he's going to have to go through me to get him."

"And me," Ollie said, taking his place beside his mother.

"And me," Everette and Levi echoed, flanking Mrs. Williams.

Adarsh stepped forward as well, folding his arms across his chest. "Me as well."

Their loyalty to Cooper had Bradford's chest tightening and him blinking back emotion. Not too much touched his heart, and he had a million questions, but he was momentarily overcome. *I'm so down with this town, as long as they don't consider killing me part of protecting Cooper.*

Chapter Twenty-Six

Amanda

TUCKED AGAINST COOPER'S side in his bed, I couldn't sleep. After checking out the Stanley house, we'd had dinner with my parents and shared our plans with them. My mother's approval had been instant. My father held back, possibly hoping to hear that Cooper had proposed, but then gave us each a hug and said he was happy for us.

I knew he was and even though he would have preferred Cooper and I were taking our relationship steps in the order he and my mother had: dating, an engagement, then marriage before pregnancy. It seemed easier for my mother to see it the way I did—the order didn't matter as long as Cooper and I ended up together.

My parents had a solid marriage based on friendship as well as love. That's what I wanted with Cooper and what I truly felt we were working toward. The proposal would come . . .

The buzz of an incoming call on my phone had me rolling over to answer it before it woke Cooper. "Tom?" I sat up, instantly concerned because he hadn't called me in years and all I could imagine was that someone we knew was hurt.

"Is Cooper with you? I need to talk to him."

Cooper's eyes opened and shifted so he was seated beside me. "Everything okay?"

Even though I was dying to know what the call was about, I handed Cooper the phone and said, "It's Tom. He wants to speak to you."

Our eyes met and held while Cooper accepted the phone. He must have seen the concern in my eyes. "Tom, I'm putting you on speakerphone."

My heart started thudding and I laced one of my hands with his free one. This—this was why I didn't care what order our relationship took.

"Okay," Tom said, "But I don't have good news."

Cooper's hand tightened on mine. "If it has to do with me, Amanda has the right to know."

God, I love him.

Tom sighed. "We have a problem. Someone came to town looking for you—"

"No," I burst out, then covered my mouth with my hand. "Sorry."

Cooper's jaw visibly tightened and between gritted teeth he demanded, "Who came looking for me? Are they still in town?"

"They are and that's the problem. Adarsh called me. It seems that he and a few people in town decided to take the law into their own hands and have the person locked in the holding cell at the old police station."

"What?" Cooper asked although I'm sure he heard Tom

as clearly as I had.

I scooted closer to Cooper, lending him my support physically as well as drawing strength from him as I tried not to panic. "Is it Clay?"

"No, but someone he sent," Tom continued. "Adarsh said he looks like a hitman. I'm heading over there now. I was going to call Simon, but I thought it was best to assess the situation before pulling him in. This is bad, Cooper. Best case, Adarsh is wrong and we find a way to convince whoever they have not to press charges for kidnapping. Worst case, your brother is sending a hitman after you and I don't know what the hell to do with that. We can't just let him go, and we have to consider the possibility that he might not be working alone."

My heart broke at the pain I saw in Cooper's eyes. It was quickly replaced, though, by panic as I felt him emotionally pulling away. "I'll meet you there, Tom."

"I'm coming," I said quickly.

"No, it's too dangerous," Cooper said as he swung his feet to the floor and stood.

"I agree," Tom added. "We have no idea how this will go down."

I rushed to my feet as well and blocked Cooper's path to his clothing. "Which is why I need to be there. I'm as much a part of this as either of you."

Cooper's eyes raged with torment. "I won't let my family take anyone else from me."

Placing my hand on his arm, I spoke my own need. "And I won't let you battle them without me, so we have a problem."

"I need you to be safe," he said in a guttural tone.

I stepped closer and touched his face gently. "There is no safe place, Cooper. Life is dangerous and temporary; the only part we control is how much we let that scare us. I'm not afraid because I know you. I know you're a good man who will somehow solve this no matter how impossible it seems—because that's who you are. You rise above what would take other people down."

"Then trust me to fix this and return to you."

I gave his arm a squeeze. "I do trust you, but ask yourself—if our roles were reversed, would you be okay with me going without you? Could you stay behind and wait to see if I come back?"

"No."

"I'll be careful." I moved my stomach. "We both have a reason to be."

He nodded and the love in his eyes made an otherwise horrible moment one that I'd always carry in my heart. "We do. Okay."

I imagined the scene we'd be walking into and added, "My parents will want to come as well." Cooper's eyebrows shot up so I added, "No matter who your brother sent, we'll face them as a family and that's why we'll win."

He pulled me to his chest, tucked my head under his chin, and shuddered. "Did you hear that, Tom? We're all coming."

"I heard," Tom said. "I guess it's fitting because my family played a role in trapping this hitman. If we go to prison, at least we all go together."

Chapter Twenty-Seven

Cooper

M Y HOPE THAT Adarsh was wrong about the type of person Clay had sent to Driverton quickly dissolved when I saw the man in the holding cell. This wasn't someone who needed to talk tough to intimidate people. There was a look in his eyes that I recognized. He'd killed in the past and would again if pushed to. The scars on his face and neck hinted at what might have driven him down that dark road.

Along with her parents, Amanda was hearing everyone else's story of what had led up to this scene. I walked directly over to face the man they called Bradford. "Who are you?"

"Bradford Wilson."

I glanced at Tom. He shrugged. "I couldn't find a record of him in any of our data bases."

Bradford said, "And you won't. That's not how I work."

Everette interrupted. "Simon wants to talk to you." He handed me his phone.

I looked over to Tom again. "I thought we weren't going to involve Simon."

Tom threw his hands up in the air. "Does it look like

anyone is listening to me?"

Point taken. I held the phone to my ear and said, "Simon. It's Cooper."

"Cooper," Simon said. "What the hell is going on there? Tell me this is a drunk prank and nothing Everette just told me is true."

I turned back to face Bradford as I spoke. "I wish I could. However, I'm looking at a Bradford Wilson locked up at the old police station and we're trying to figure out what the hell to do now."

"Did you say Wilson?"

"Yes."

"No. It can't be who I'm thinking. Is he an unusually tall man? Scars all over his face? Mean looking?"

"You know him?"

"If he's who I think he is, we're both in a lot of trouble. I've never met him, but I've heard about him. He's with the CIA not the FBI . . . and he's kind of a legend."

"The CIA?" I nodded toward Bradford. "You work for them?"

Bradford folded his arms across his chest. "I do."

Amanda came to stand beside me, slipping her hand into mine. "I don't care if he's the president, you've done nothing wrong, Cooper. He can't touch you."

"We do have him locked in a cell," Cooper said.

"I did that," Mrs. Williams said. "And I'd do it again."

"Technically, I did it," Adarsh said. "But I didn't know he was with the government when I did."

"Simon, how dangerous is this man?"

"In general? Extremely? In your case, I don't know. I'm sorry. I'm driving to Driverton now. I wouldn't release him until we know what he's doing there."

"Understood. How far out are you?"

"About an hour."

"You know where we are." I ended the call.

Along with Pete, Dotty came over to where we were standing. She spoke to Bradford while pointing to me. "Before you do or say anything, you should know that Cooper acted in self-defense. I'd look into how everyone else in his family died before asking if what he did to his uncle was justified."

Pete put his arms around his wife. "Dotty, I'm not sure that's helping."

She protested, "He's CIA, you don't think he knows about the uncle?"

Levi joined them. "Maybe not. He could be here because of the sex trafficker Cooper killed."

Everette added, "That's all old news. It's more likely the CIA would care about the stuff Cooper has been doing with Tom."

Bradford frowned. "Tom?"

Mrs. Williams joined them. "Sheriff Tom. My nephew is the only law that matters around here. If you're here to stop the two of them from finding runaways and kidnapped children, there's a special place for you in hell and I'll help you get there."

Tom jumped in, "Stop. Although we appreciate all the support, you're all going to land Cooper and me in jail if you don't zip it."

"If anyone is going to be arrested for all of this, it's me. Just me." I needed to make that clear.

Bradford raised both hands and it was only then that I realized he was more than a little inebriated. "I'm not here to arrest anyone, so please stop confessing. Clay sent me to find you."

That didn't make me feel much better. "Why? Why now? What does he want?"

Bradford shrugged. "I'm curious, how did you get your uncle's body to Brazil?"

"I don't know what you're talking about." I didn't.

"Did you withdraw yourself from school?"

"I ran and kept running." I glanced down at Amanda. "Until I found somewhere safe."

She wrapped her arms around my waist. "That's how I feel as well."

Bradford pinched the bridge of his nose. "I'm way too drunk for this. If you're going to kill me, do it now while I won't feel a thing."

"No one is going to kill anyone," Pete said firmly.

"That's not who we are," I said, emotion tightening my throat. "Not who I ever should have been."

Tom put a hand on my shoulder. "I haven't had a chance to tell you, but I tracked down the other two boys who were there the night you shot your kidnapper. They're not only grateful for what you did for them, but they worked with the authorities and because of what you did, they were able to track down the others the couple had taken and save them as well."

Amanda held me tighter. "It's time to stop loathing yourself for doing what you had to. Look around Cooper. If you have any doubt left about who you are, look around, we don't."

I took a moment to confirm what I knew she'd said out of love and was humbled by the unwavering loyalty in the eyes of my Driverton family. It was in that moment that I realized why I fought so hard for those I saw as powerless—because I'd known that feeling for the first sixteen years of my life. A part of me had held to the belief that no matter what I did or who I saved, there was no one coming to save me.

But there they were—not all of them sober, but this was my calvary. It was time to stop hating the child I'd been and doubting the man I could be. I was more than the worst I'd ever been. I could be a good father, husband, son, friend, neighbor. "Thank you."

"Okay," Bradford said. "You've convinced me . . . I need to live here at least part-time. I'll buy the Stanley house."

"No." The word was voiced by not only me, but those around me. I smiled then met Amanda's gaze. "Amanda and I are going to buy it, get married, and fill it with kids."

She was all smiles and tears. "That's the plan."

Mrs. Williams cut in, "I didn't hear a proposal."

Amanda laughed. "I didn't either, but that's why I know it'll happen." She wiped at her cheek then turned to address the group. "He's already promised to change half the diapers."

"That's better than a ring," Dotty said cheerfully. "Partnership is the best foundation for a marriage."

Pete hugged her closer. "I agree."

Levi said, "There's the Bentley place just outside of town. The house is crap, but it has a hundred or so acres. It'd be pretty sweet for a horse rescue."

When all eyes turned to him, Levi shrugged. "Obviously, only if Bradford turns out to not be a hitman." When no one said anything, he added defensively, "Sure, look at me like that, but I had fun with him."

Everette nodded reluctantly. "I did too."

Not meeting anyone's gaze, Ollie added, "I did feel bad locking him up." He turned to Bradford. "Everyone makes mistakes, Bradford. It's not too late to turn your life around."

Bradford took out his phone. "I need to make a call."

"Don't let him do it," Mrs. Williams said.

Tom shook his head at his aunt. "There's not too much we can do to stop him."

She looked less convinced.

Amanda gave me a squeeze. "Whatever happens—"

"We face it together," I finished for her and kissed her gently. *Life is dangerous and temporary; the only part we control is how much we let that scare us.*

"Ian," Bradford said loud enough for us all to hear. "I'm in Driverton. Yes, I found Cooper. I'm with him now. He has a good life here. If you haven't found anything to convince me otherwise, I say we need to fully investigate what role Clay played in all of this before we say anything about Cooper."

Amanda let out a shaky breath.

I felt some of my tension abate as well. Bradford didn't sound like someone who'd come to arrest or erase me.

"I didn't expect less from you," he said. "What did you uncover? The grandmother? Interesting. That makes sense." He listened for a minute more then met my gaze and said, "My friend has been looking into what happened to your uncle. It appears your grandmother cleaned up the scene and shipped his body off to Brazil."

"Why would she? She didn't want anything to do with me."

Bradford continued, "I wouldn't say your grandmother would win an award for being nurturing, but I doubt she knew what Ryssen was up to. Your grandfather had dementia at the end of his life. All of her attention went there. I believe that's what allowed Ryssen to get away with what he did."

"Like kill my parents?" I asked in disgust.

Bradford shrugged. "I have no idea if their accident was your uncle's fault, but I do know that when they died your grandmother brought Clay over to help her with your grandfather. If anything Clay says is true, your uncle deliberately distanced you, Caterina, and Collin from him and your grandmother so no one would suspect he was spending your money. Clay was told you wanted nothing to do with him. It was only when Caterina reached out to Clay that he realized your uncle had kept you away from each other as part of a dark plan."

"Caterina?" My sister's name caught in my throat.

Amanda's soft protest brought my attention to how my hands had tightened on her. I softened my hold as my body began to shake with emotion and hope. "She's alive? I thought she was dead."

"That was likely how she would have ended up had your uncle lived," Bradford said matter-of-factly.

Amanda brought her hands up to cup my face. "See why you're my hero? You saved your sister as well."

Tears filled my eyes. I took her hands in mine and lowered them, but whispered, "I love you," before turning to Bradford. I wanted to believe him so badly it hurt. "Show me proof."

"My phone is full of photos of her at the farm. My wife takes a lot of photos." Without ending the call, he turned his phone toward me and through the bars of the holding cell showed me my sister, older than I remembered her, but happy and most importantly alive. Bradford swiped to show more photos of her. "The man she's with is Benjamin Drover, her fiancé. They've spent a lot of time at our farm as they get to know Clay. We're their safe place."

This time a tear escaped and rolled down my cheeks as I looked around at the people I loved who all looked emotionally invested in the news. As if they might have missed the reveal, I said, "My sister's alive. She's really alive."

Amanda and Dotty hugged me then each other. Tom did as well, then stepped back and wiped at his own wet cheeks. Blinking quickly, he gave my shoulder a smack, smiled, and sniffed. Everette burst into tears which first made Ollie and Levi laugh then get all teary with him.

Adarsh was the most composed, but he was smiling.

In a stern voice, Mrs. Williams said, "I only cry at funerals and this is the opposite of one." She took the keys off the desktop and opened the holding cell door. "I'm glad we didn't have to kill you, Bradford Wilson."

"Me too," Bradford said in a light tone.

From the phone, Ian asked, "Did I just hear someone say they were going to kill you? What's happening up there?"

"Nothing bad." Bradford stepped out of the cell. "I'm just falling in love with a whole damn town."

"Are you drunk?" Ian asked.

"Yes," Bradford laughed and punched Levi in the arm. "But so are my friends."

Levi's smile was ridiculously bright and the mood of the group lightened. "I knew you liked us."

"You have friends in Driverton?" Ian asked, clearly confused.

Mrs. Williams walked up to Bradford and nodded. "He does now. But that doesn't mean you can stay at my place without doing chores. And if you can get Ollie to fix the back fence I'll send you home with the best berry pie you ever tasted."

"Mom, I'm going to fix the fence," Ollie protested. "I've been busy at the pub."

I nodded toward Ollie then the others. "What do you say we get it done this weekend? Together."

Ollie nodded as did the others.

"I'm in," Bradford said. "And if you want, I can have Clay and Caterina here helping as well."

I whipped around.

Amanda's hand found mine.

The idea of Clay coming to Driverton could either be exciting or something I needed to prepare a defense for. I put my arm around Amanda and took a moment to choose my reaction. Fear was a choice. "I'm not sixteen anymore. If Clay brings trouble here . . ."

Bradford made a face. "Clay isn't the kind of trouble you'll have any idea what to do with." I didn't have time to think much about that claim before he added, "He's going to try to do a lot of things for you. He has a difficult time understanding that he doesn't have to buy friendship."

"I don't want his money," I said with conviction.

"Technically, a third of his money is yours," Bradford said. "And before you say you don't need it, you and I should talk. Ian, if I'm right about what Cooper has been up to with his buddy Tom, our team might be expanding."

Tom asked, "Your team? Are you asking him to join the CIA?"

Bradford gave him a long look then me. "Yes and no. When Ian comes up, the four of us will talk."

Although I had no idea what he was referring to, I felt compelled to add, "If it's the kind of job that requires loyalty and integrity, we should include Everette."

Everette stood taller and smiled.

Ollie said, "If I can do it while I run the pub, I'm interested as well."

Levi volunteered, "I'll bring the moonshine."

When Mrs. Williams made a tsk sound, Levi added,

"What? You don't think people in the CIA love moonshine? Bradford loved it."

She laughed and several of the others joined in.

I met Amanda's gaze. Everything was about to change—again. "My brother is coming here."

She nodded slowly, searching my face for my feelings on the matter. I fell even more in love with her then. Another person might have been wondering what that would mean for themselves or been excited about the prospect of having access to the kind of money that might come their way. Amanda's focus was on me and her support was unwavering. Her faith in me had me standing taller and suddenly confident that there wasn't a scenario Clay could bring that we couldn't handle—together. I vowed then to do all I could to deserve that kind of love.

I gently caressed one of her cheeks. "I'm going to marry you, Amanda Glenford."

Her smile beamed. "That's the plan."

"Our first official date might have to wait until after we say 'I do' because I don't want to wait."

"I'd be disappointed if we did it any other way."

Our kiss was full of friendship, passion, love, and promises—everything we were to each other—and so damn intense I didn't want it to ever end. That it had to end was survivable only because I knew I'd have forever with the woman in my arms.

Chapter Twenty-Eight

Amanda

A S A TEEN, I'd suspected Cooper had feelings for me, but even then I'd never allowed myself to believe we could have anything as strong and beautiful as this. Our lives were complicated but our love wasn't.

We didn't follow social norms, didn't worry about what others might think of us. When he raised his head and smiled down at me I saw our future in his eyes—a house full of family, friends, and laughter. Life would throw challenges our way, but we would be each other's strength.

I had a true partner.

A best friend.

As I searched his face, an idea came to me. "The weekend is four days away." When he cocked his head in question, I continued, "I could plan a wedding in that time."

His eyebrows rose.

The more I thought about it, the more I liked the idea. "We probably should wait until after you've reunited with your brother and sister and everything is settled, but that's not our style."

A chuckled rumbled out of him. "It definitely isn't. Let's do it."

"Get married this weekend?"

He answered first with a deep kiss that left me breathless, then a husky: "Hell, yes."

From somewhere behind me, Mrs. Williams asked, "Did she just propose?"

Bradford was the one who answered, "Who actually asked first is a little murky."

My father said, "Dotty, are you up to throwing a wedding together in less than a week?"

The excitement in my mother's voice said it all. "Up to it? This is the stuff I'm sticking around for." With a laugh and a light tap to my father's cheek, she added, "And to be with you, of course."

He pulled her to him, gave her a little spin in his arms then kissed her. "If I'm competing with a wedding, I'll have to up my game."

All smiles, she said, "I'd say you have nothing to worry about, but I do love it when you bring it."

The spark of desire in my father's eyes was enough to have me quickly looking away. "I can't. Those are my parents."

Cooper chuckled again and hugged me to his chest. "And hopefully us when we're that old."

Both of my parents turned to me and Cooper in mock outrage. My mother said, "Did he just call us old?"

My father arched an eyebrow in jest at Cooper. "He wouldn't dare because he knows I'd retaliate by bringing a shotgun to the wedding."

"A shotgun wedding? Dad, really?"

The look my parents gave each other before they both started laughing warmed me from head to toe. They were each other's ride or die, partner in crime. And I loved it.

Hand over her mouth as if trying to stem her laughter, my mother said, "Can you imagine? Knowing how people view small-towners like us, his family would believe it."

Laughing so hard his eyes were watering, my father added, "We could make up all kinds of 'traditions' and pass them off as normal."

Levi joined them. "I watched a frog hopping competition on YouTube. You could give everyone a bullfrog as a wedding favor and we could race them at the reception."

Everette's face lit up. "And pretend we always do that."

Ollie rubbed his chin. "Everyone would have to be in on the joke or it wouldn't be funny." He turned to Bradford. "You're our only weak link. Pick a side. You one of us?"

Before Bradford had a chance to respond, Levi gave his back a pat. "You just have to look surprised."

Mrs. Williams made a sound. "Boys, you are not ruining Amanda and Cooper's wedding with a prank."

I looked up at Cooper. In a tone low enough that I hoped only he could hear, I said, "It's your family the prank would be on."

He searched my face. "Your opinion is the only one that matters in this. What do you want?"

"Beyond you?"

His grin was instant. "Yes, because that's a done deal."

I glanced around and imagined two versions of the day. The first one was picture perfect, magazine suitable, expensive, and traditional. The other was a group effort, hilarious and potentially a real shitshow. "How would your family respond to a bullfrog race?"

His expression turned more serious. "I have no idea."

"They might not like it."

"I don't care what they do or don't like."

If that was true, I hoped it wouldn't always be. "If we reveal the joke in a way that doesn't embarrass them, it might be a fun way to break the ice with them."

"Don't agree to it for me. I want it to be a special day for you."

Right there was one of the million reasons I loved him. "I want the same for you." After looking into his eyes for a few minutes, I said, "I love when you laugh, Cooper. Does a bullfrog race sound as funny to you as it does to me?"

He nodded. "It does, actually. I'm not looking forward to rehashing the past with Clay and Caterina. I'm glad my sister is alive, but we don't have a lot of happy memories. I don't know that I ever shared a laugh with Clay. If we did the bullfrog prank right, maybe that would change."

That sold me on the idea. "Let's do it. Let's give the town and your siblings a funny, shared memory. We'll welcome them, Driverton style—make them one of us." I looked around. "Levi. Ollie. Everette," I said to call their attention to me. "We can't do this alone. I'm thinking one bullfrog per family. You think you could organize catching enough? And then someone would have to take care of them until we bring them out at the reception."

Everette volunteered, "We'll keep them at our house. My brothers and sisters can keep them fed and healthy until we need them then release them in a pond after the race."

Tom nudged Ollie. "Ollie and I will design and build a portable racetrack, something we can roll out on the lawn of wherever you have the wedding."

Since the Stanley house was far from ready, I looked at my parents and asked, "If we do all the work, could we use your backyard?"

My mother smiled. "That's always been the dream."

My father turned to Adarsh and asked, "Could we hire you to cater it?"

"Hire? No," Adarsh said. "We cater for free as a gift or we don't cater." He and my father shook hands warmly.

Levi said, "I'll make the . . ."

I knew what he was going to say and resigned myself to the fact that few would be sober at my wedding.

"Wedding arbor," he finished. "Tell me the kind of flowers you like, Amanda. Keep in mind, though, that Mrs. Williams's rose bushes are in bloom and if she said yes those would be free."

I chuckled. "My favorite flower is whatever you can get your hands on, Levi, thank you."

"I suppose it would be for a good cause," Mrs. Williams puffed up with pride. "And I do grow better roses than you could ever find in a shop."

My mother chimed in, "That's what everyone has always said."

"Done," Mrs. Williams said. "Also, Adarsh, I'd like to help with the catering. You'll need extra hands."

"We'll all pitch in," my father promised. "That's what family does."

The door of the police station opened and slammed shut a moment before a flustered-looking Simon rushed into the room. His mouth rounded in surprise as he took in the scene. "You let him out."

"Yes." Cooper walked over to greet him with a handshake. "Thank you for coming and for everything."

Simon nodded toward Bradford. "Is he drunk?"

"Probably," Cooper said.

"Not as much as I was." Bradford approached, not looking nearly as friendly as he had a moment before. "And you are?"

Simon cleared his throat. "Simon Tull. I'm Everette's cousin and"—he let out a breath before continuing—"FBI."

"No one's perfect," Bradford said.

Simon loosened his tie. "Not sure what you're doing here, Mr. Wilson, but this is a good town full of good people."

"I believe you," Bradford said, then with a completely straight face, he added, "and that's why I've decided to take up bullfrog racing. I hear it's a popular, competitive sport in these parts. I'll be coming in as a novice, but I'm confident I'll quickly acquire the necessary skills."

Simon looked around in confusion. "What is he talking about?"

I laced my hand with Cooper's. "Cooper and I are getting married this weekend."

"In our backyard," my father interjected.

Tom said, "So, of course, the reception will include Driverton's traditional wedding bullfrog race."

"Have you all been smoking again?" Simon asked.

Bradford frowned, looking convincingly irritated and confused. "Are you implying such a race is not really a thing?"

Simon blinked once or twice then cleared his throat again, stalling as he assessed the situation again. "I'm implying nothing, just asking questions."

Bradford's eyes narrowed. "You realize you could lose your career over what happened here today?"

After swallowing visibly, Simon said, "Family is worth it."

Everette walked over to hug him, followed by Mrs. Williams and Ollie.

Only then did Bradford smile. "I like you and I like your family. I need to step outside to make some phone calls, but after we can move the fridge, then talk."

"I don't actually need the fridge," Mrs. Williams said.

Bradford shot her a comically shocked look. "You lied to me."

She shrugged. "You weren't yet one of us."

He nodded, then smiled, looked around and smiled more. "I mean it, Joanna and I will buy a house around here, even if only to vacation in. You didn't try to kill me, and that means a lot to me."

Cooper straightened. "Will one of those calls be to my

brother?"

"Yes."

"I'd like to be there for that one," Cooper said. I didn't ask if I could be there, because I didn't want to push, but he gave my hand a light squeeze and said, "We'd both like to."

Bradford nodded once. "Okay. Give me a few minutes to talk to my wife and explain to her that our plans for the weekend have changed, then we'll make that call."

My happiness could not be contained. I left Cooper's side briefly to give Bradford a tight hug that seemed to take him completely by surprise. When he stepped back he retrieved his gun from the desk, but smiled as he made his way out of the room.

"I can't believe that's Bradford Wilson," Simon said.

"I can." I took the hand Cooper held out to me. "This town brings out the best in people."

"I may even stop drinking," Levi said. When we all turned toward him, he added, "Maybe. I still need to test the stuff I make, but I could cut down."

"We all could," Ollie said. "Who knows, sober I might even win at darts." He waved a hand at Everette.

Everette opened his mouth to likely voice a little jab, glanced at Mrs. Williams, paused, then said, "I bet you could. We're all capable of more. It's time to find out what that looks like."

"There's no longer a need for me to list eligible men for Amanda, but I've heard Mary Singer is still single and considering moving back to the area," Mrs. Williams said.

"You wouldn't," Levi said.

"That depends on you, Levi," Mrs. Williams said in a prim voice. "I'm sure she'll come home for the wedding. I'll give you until after that."

"Mrs. Williams." Cooper said her name in a playful tone.

She turned to him with a hand on one hip. "Yes?"

"Don't ever change. I love you just the way you are." He tilted his head toward me and winked. "You may have to share my heart."

I wrapped an arm around his waist, slipping my hand into his back pocket possessively. "As long as it's just your heart," I joked.

He slid a hand into my back pocket and gave my cheek a light squeeze. "Is that how it's going to be?"

Going up onto my tiptoes, I murmured against his lips, "That's how it's going to be."

The world had never felt so right.

Mrs. Williams laughed. "You two. How did it take you so long to see what the rest of us knew all along?"

While basking in the love shining in Cooper's eyes, I marveled that the expression wasn't new. "I have no idea. I've been in love with Cooper pretty much since the first time we met."

He brought his free hand up to run through my hair. "It was the same for me."

Whoosh, I fell for him even more.

In the background, Levi said, "So, Mary could be in love with me but hiding it?"

"Hiding it really, really well," Ollie said, then added, "you're right, anything is possible."

I looked around the room—from my smiling parents to a suddenly friendly-looking Bradford and agreed. No one would believe me if we told them how we'd gotten to this place, but somehow it worked. I glanced up at Cooper and said, "Let's go call your family."

He glanced down at my stomach then met my gaze again. "*Our* family."

"Yes." *No matter what they bring to the table, good or bad, they are blood related to my baby so they'll always be part of me as well.*

Here's hoping they're only as crazy as everyone else I know.

Chapter Twenty-Nine

Cooper

IF SOMEONE HAD told me I'd one day be standing in the breakroom of the old police station, holding Amanda's hand, while waiting for a complete stranger who was still sobering up from partying with my friends to inform my brother of my location, I would have dismissed their claim as beyond impossible.

But there I was.

"Ready?" Bradford asked in a surprising show of empathy.

I glanced at Amanda, saw nothing but love and hope in her eyes, and nodded. "Call him."

Bradford touched the screen of his phone to initiate a video call. Clay didn't pick up on the first beep, the second, or the third. Bradford rolled his eyes skyward. "I'll call his wife." He ended the first call and chose another number.

I couldn't see the screen of his phone from where I was, but a female voice answered in a loud whisper. "Bradford, Clay's sleeping. Is it important?"

Bradford didn't answer, but the expression on his face

was clear enough.

Rather than sounding intimidated, she chided, "Don't give me that look. I know everything with you is important, but Clay hasn't slept well since he found out about how his uncle had treated Caterina. He's worried something might have also happened to Cooper. If I wake him up and tell him you're on the phone he's going to assume it's with news about Cooper. Is it?" Her voice lowered. "And if it is, is he alive?" She took an audible deep breath. "And if he's alive, is he okay or did his uncle send him away somewhere awful as well? Oh, God, I haven't slept in weeks either. Some therapist is going to make a lot of money off me when this is over."

There was a softening of Bradford's expression. "This is regarding Cooper."

"You found him?" she asked in a rush.

"I did."

"I'll get Clay," she said breathlessly. "Don't hang up."

"I'm not going anywhere." Bradford muted his phone, met my gaze, and said, "Your brother and his wife, Lexi, are . . . high strung. I could introduce you, but it'd be better for you to take my phone and talk to him yourself."

I took the phone he held out to me. The camera was darkened, as if it were placed against something and the sound was off. I tipped it toward Amanda so she could see as well. "She must have put the phone down."

The camera shot changed to the wall and then a face that shared some of my features, but was older, and more polished than mine. His hair was in disarray from sleep, but cut in a modern style and he was wearing what looked like a silk bathrobe. "Clay," I said. "It's Cooper."

The camera showed another shot of a wall, then the carpet before Lexi's face appeared on again. "Clay dropped the phone. Here he is again."

This time when Clay's face filled the screen his eyes were wide and he was pale. "Cooper? Is that really you? Hold on, Lexi, can you wake the nanny? Boppy will need to go out." There was a flash of fur across the screen. "Sorry, our dog makes mistakes in the house when he's woken at night."

"A nanny? You have children," I said, not sure how I felt about that. On one hand I had a nephew or a niece and that was something to celebrate. On the other hand, it was sad that I had no idea how old they were or anything at all about them.

"No," he said before turning his camera so I could also see his wife's face. "Lexi and I are trying, but so far all we have is Boppy."

"Your dog?"

"Yes. Boppy, our dog. He's a Havanese. They have to be brushed daily, require weekly baths. I couldn't imagine not having help with that."

"To brush your dog." I couldn't process that. Who the hell had a nanny for their dog?

Clay moved the phone. "Do we have a bad connection? Sorry, am I cutting out?"

I glanced at Bradford as I remembered all the times I'd worried Clay had been behind the deaths in my family. I'd imagined him as an intimidating, large man with the same evil in his eyes that I'd seen in my uncle's.

This was Clay?

This is what I'd hidden from?

I could kick his ass blindfolded with my arms tied be-hind my back.

I remembered the bullfrog race prank and wondered if there'd be any time for Bradford to arrange for something similar from Clay, but I couldn't recall him walking away from the group. "Is this a fucking joke?" I demanded.

Amanda put a hand on my chest and leaned toward the phone. "Hi. My name is Amanda. It's a pleasure to meet both of you."

They both introduced themselves to her. Their exchange gave me time to pin Bradford down with a pointed look.

In a low tone, he said, "No, that's your brother."

I shook my head. It didn't seem possible.

Still looking a little dazed, Clay said, "I promised Cateri-na I'd tell her as soon as we found you. Do you mind if I add her to this call? She's going to be so excited."

He'd done it before I had a chance to answer him. A sec-ond image appeared, splitting the screen with Clay's video. I knew that face and that smile. "Caterina." My voice was hoarse.

Her hand flew to her mouth. "Cooper? Is that really you? Clay, you found him."

"Technically, Bradford did," Clay said cheerfully, "but yes, we found him."

"Benjamin, come here," Caterina called out. "It's Cooper. It's my little brother." Her eyes filled with tears.

"I've looked for you for so long, Cooper. If you're angry with me for something, just know that I love you so much. Not a day went by when I didn't think about you and hope you were somewhere safe."

My throat clogged with emotion. "I'm safe. I'm sorry I didn't tell you that. I thought you were dead." The excuse sounded as shitty out loud as it felt to admit. "I shouldn't have believed anything our uncle said. I should have looked for you. I love you too." I did. She was the one who'd made sure Collin and I had a relationship. She was the only one who'd ever fought for our family. "Our uncle said he'd taken care of you the same way he'd taken care of our parents and Collin. What did that mean?"

Her face tightened. "That's a story for another time, Cooper." She cleared her throat. "But for now, there's someone I want you to meet. Cooper, this is Benjamin, my fiancé."

A man's face appeared beside hers. "Nice to meet you, Cooper."

"Hello." After a pause, I brought Amanda back on camera with me. "I called to invite both of you . . . all of you . . . to our wedding this Saturday. I realize it's short notice, but we would love to have you join us."

"A wedding?" Clay asked, his tone rising. "I not only love weddings, but I'm also really good at throwing them together. Ask Bradford. You bring the love—I bring the magic. And the champagne."

"No," I said with more force than I'd meant to.

Amanda's hand tightened on mine.

I started over. "Thank you, but no. We're having a traditional small-town wedding. Nothing fancy. But, if you'd like to join us, I'll send you the information."

"We'd love to come," Caterina said with enthusiasm.

"Oh, nothing could keep me away, but I do think you should at least consider letting me add a little flair to whatever you have planned. I don't want to brag, but I've gotten rather good at wedding planning."

Lexi covered Clay's mouth with her hand. "What Clay is saying is that we'd love to come as well. If you need anything we're here for you. If you want us to simply show up, we can do that as well. We're just glad we found you and we're grateful to be invited."

Clay removed her hand from his mouth and seemed about to say something then frowned. I had no idea what he'd say next. Before speaking he gave Lexi's hand a light kiss. "Thank you. You're right, this isn't about me." He straightened. "Caterina and I have only recently started talking. Before that, all I was ever told was that none of you wanted anything to do with me. I believed those lies." He expelled a loud breath. "And because of that, I was never the brother I should have been. I didn't protect you because I didn't pay attention enough to know that you required protection. I looked for you, but never as hard as I should have. To be honest, I probably didn't want to find you. I knew—or I thought I knew—what you thought of me and I didn't want to face that." His face contorted. "I had no idea you were not being taken care of. I thought I was making the right choices, taking care of our grandparents, doing the best

I could to be a good person. I thought you were ungrateful, spiteful, and mean just as our uncle always was. He talked about the three of you like you were living the perfect life away from me. Together. I've asked myself a thousand times how different all of our lives would have been had I chosen to not believe him—had I sought you out on my own."

"I wasn't nice to you the time you tried," Caterina said. "And I've come to terms with the role I played in what happened to me as well. We were all duped, all manipulated, and all hurt even if it was in different ways."

A long silence followed that. Amanda was the first to speak. "It saddens me that your uncle hurt so many people, but selfishly, a piece of me can't hate how it brought Cooper into my life. He has been so good to me, so good to my family and to everyone in our town."

I bent and gave her temple a kiss. "I know what you're saying. I'm not glad I went through any of it, but I am grateful it brought me here . . . to you."

Lexi kissed Clay on the cheek. "Love is a healing power. Clay's tearing himself up over what happened to both of you, but your uncle doesn't have the power to keep you apart anymore. You can decide to forgive each other and become a family again."

Caterina sniffed. "It's what I've always wanted."

"Me too," Clay said, his voice thick with emotion.

I had to be honest. "I'd given up on that as a possibility. Caterina, I believed you were gone. And Clay, I have no good memories of you. Not one. We came out of the same people, but does that make us a family?" Amanda laid her head on my shoulder and simply held me close.

There was another long pause, then Clay said, "You don't remember Captain Red Cape and the Pirates of the Sand?"

"I don't," I said, but an image of a red cape flashed through my mind.

Clay continued, "I was probably eleven. Collin was nine. Caterina, you were young. Six maybe? And Cooper you were little. Three, maybe four? We had a huge wooden ship in a playground that had sand as footing. I took a red tablecloth from the kitchen staff and made myself a cape. Collin and Caterina wanted to be pirates."

"I was a dolphin," I said as the memory resurfaced.

Clay laughed. "Yes. We never really understood why. I suggested you be a shark so you could at least eat the pirates when I had them walk the plank."

Caterina added, "But you didn't want to hurt anyone, Cooper. You wanted to be something fast and strong enough to save us if we fell into the sand."

"I remember that," I said slowly. I could hear the laughter we'd shared while playing that game. I could almost feel the warmth of the sand beneath my bare feet. "We didn't play it just once."

"No, it was your favorite game and we used to have fun together," Clay said. His smile faded. "All that ended when Mom and Dad died. I was only twelve when our grandparents sent for me."

"Twelve. You were a child." I'd always imagined him older. "I always thought you chose them over us, but you didn't really have a choice, did you?"

"I didn't," Clay said. "And before you envy me for having been raised there, it wasn't ideal. I'm probably as messed up as the two of you—no offense, Caterina."

She smiled and rolled her eyes. "I agree, so none taken."

Clay added, "I didn't know what a real friend was until I met Lexi." His wife leaned closer against him. "So sometimes I try too hard, but only because I know what it's like to be alone, really alone, and I don't ever want to be that again."

Lexi rested her head against his cheek. "Oh, hon. You won't be."

Amanda wiped at one of her cheeks. "Don't give up on each other. This is hard, but I have to believe you're all past the worst of it. Now you can help each other heal."

"That sounds like more than I was signing on for," I joked even though I was half-serious.

Bradford coughed.

Caterina nodded. "I wasn't sure if having Clay in my life was worth reopening the past, but I know now that it is. Forgiving him, forgiving myself, took away the power that my memories had over me. I've been able to let go of the anger and fear and that has freed me to start a life with Benjamin." She looked at her fiancé. "I can finally be me."

Free.

That's what I finally was.

Amanda smiled up at me. "That's what you want, isn't it, Cooper?"

To lighten the intensity of the moment, I joked, "To be with Benjamin?"

She lightly slapped my chest. "Yes, that's what I meant."

She was right, but that didn't feel like the time to go into how good it would feel to be free to be myself. In a more serious tone, I said, "So Saturday, if you're all available, you're officially invited to our wedding."

"We'll be there," Caterina answered.

"We will be as well," Clay said. He looked away from the camera and made a face. "Boppy, no. He wet the rug. I'll wake the staff."

"The staff?" I asked in amusement. "You know, you could clean it up yourself."

Clay gave me a look as if he were trying to translate what I'd said into a language he understood, then shook his head and said he'd see us on Saturday. Caterina promised to be there early and the call ended.

I handed the phone back to Bradford. "So, that's Clay."

Bradford pocketed his phone and smiled. "That's Clay."

I met Amanda's gaze and said, "I have nothing in common with him."

She pressed her lips together as if searching for the right thing to say.

Bradford added, "I feel the same, but I do know that he means well. So, if you want to make him happy, let him do something for the wedding. If you don't, he'll try to surprise you and trust me that's always worse."

Amanda snapped her fingers in the air. "We could have him work with Mrs. Williams and Levi on the decorations."

Bradford made a sound then shook his head.

"Why shouldn't we?" I asked.

"Sorry," Bradford said, "I was thinking about something else, but it's too mean."

"Mean?" Amanda cocked her head to one side.

"Not so much mean . . . stupid? Forget it."

"Okay, now I'm curious," I said.

Bradford brought a fist up to his forehead. "I can't believe I'm going to say this, but it would be fucking hilarious if you told Clay that Mrs. Williams is the town matchmaker. He thinks he's the reason why everyone around him has paired up. It's ridiculous, but if you want to see your brother in all his glory tell him that she's trying to get Levi and Mary together but so far has been unsuccessful and then stand back and watch."

"Instead of the bullfrog race?" Amanda asked.

"Oh, no, you have to do that too. I need to see if Clay faints when he touches a frog."

"You have a dark side," I said, wagging a finger at Bradford. "But I like it."

"A dark side," Bradford said with a flash of teeth. "You have no idea."

Amanda clapped her hands together. "That sounds like a topic for another night. We have a wedding to plan, only four days to do it, and I need a dress. Priorities."

I swung her around and smiled down at her. "Mrs. Landon. I do like how that sounds."

"Me too." She rose to her tiptoes to kiss me and Bradford discreetly left the room.

Chapter Thirty

Cooper

A FEW DAYS later, dressed in a button-down shirt and black slacks, I stood beside a rose-covered arbor in the Glenford's backyard. Dotty and Pete were sitting in the front row of an area of folded white chairs. Seated to their left were Clay and his wife. Caterina and her fiancé were to the right of Amanda's parents. Braford and his wife were in the row behind along with Levi, Ollie, and the others. Pretty much everyone in town had shown up. It seemed fitting that they were mixed together.

What an odd couple of days we'd had . . .

I knew my family was wealthy but that hadn't prepared me for the caravan of high-tech, two-story, multi-bedroom mansions on wheels they'd arrived in. With the permission of the Stanley family, we'd sent the line of eighteen wheelers to one of the fields beside the old house.

That they'd brought their own living areas made sense. They wanted to stay in town, there weren't enough empty bedrooms at Mrs. Williams's house and they didn't want to be separated. Clay had arranged for not only a mobile home for Lexi and him, but also one for Caterina and Benjamin, another for Bradford and Joanna, still another for Amanda and me, and even one for Dotty and Pete so we could all be together in a large circle of portable homes.

Gaudy. Over the top. Completely unnecessary, but also incredibly thoughtful. After a brief uncomfortable period where the Glenfords and I tried not to be amazed at how many gadgets a mobile home could have as well as how it expanded both upward and outward, it was really nice to have time together.

What I enjoyed the most was watching Amanda and her parents guide my family through what otherwise might have been a painful reunion. Pete introduced Clay to Mrs. Williams, the perfection of her pies, as well as how our town relied more on trading services rather than money.

Within hours several less elaborate mobile homes rolled into town with construction crews that Clay sent to stay with Mrs. Williams. By the end of the first day, she had a new roof, her house had a fresh coat of paint, and her yard had never looked so good. By the end of the second day Pete and Dotty's backyard was wedding ready.

The day before the wedding, I'd taken Caterina aside and asked, "Exactly how rich is Clay?"

She'd made a strange face. "I haven't found anyone who knows for certain, but that's true of you and me as well. We inherited everything in equal parts. It's dispersed globally and in every currency. There are properties, shares in companies, stockpiles of gold. Not only did our grandparents know how to diversify their portfolio, but Clay has managed the growth of our wealth. I've spoken with some top finan-cial advisors, and they're amazed when they see that Clay isn't nearly as passive as he appears. On the outside he seems frivolous and impulsive, but behind the scenes he protected our inheritance and even grew it for us." She waved her hand in the direction of the luxury mobile homes. "This is more than I need, but Benjamin and I are looking for ways to use our money for the betterment of humanity. It's a big respon-sibility and the first ideas we had weren't practical, but we're figuring it out. At first, all you think you should do is give it away, because you feel guilty. But then you start to see ways you can be strategic with those resources and help people in all walks of life—here and abroad. It's a lot to take in, but if there's something you're passionate about, you now have nearly unlimited resources to make it happen."

"Holy shit."

She'd placed a hand on my arm. "Everything comes with a price. You'll have to hire security. When you meet new people, you'll wonder if they like you or want something from you." She smiled. "And you might have to get a cell phone."

"Now you're talking crazy," I said lightly while I ab-sorbed the enormity of how my life would change. "Bradford wants to introduce Tom and me to Ian Barrington. He said something about joining their team."

"The Barringtons are a good family. They've sort of adopted Clay and have been amazing to me. I don't know exactly what Bradford and Ian do, but from what I hear it's everything you'd agree with. I'd at least meet him and hear them out."

After a moment, I'd nodded toward the Stanley house in the distance. "None of this changes my plan to live here with Amanda."

She'd glanced at the house then tilted her head to one side. "I have an idea for a surprise you could give Amanda for a wedding present."

"A wedding present?" With everything that had gone on, I hadn't thought of that. My tone sounded annoyed, but it was with myself and not her.

She'd raised her hands nervously. "I'm sorry. It was just a thought. Some people do that."

I hated how easily she backed down from any show of aggression because it hinted at how my uncle had hurt her as well. "No, I'm sorry. I'd love to hear your idea."

A smile had returned to her face, "I was thinking about tomorrow and how we'll be at the Glenford's all day . . . after seeing what Clay's people were able to do in one day at Mrs. Williams's house, I started to think. I know you don't own the Stanley house yet. We've both experienced the downside to having money, but there are some perks. I'm not as good at it as Clay is, but if we worked with him on how to get it done, I'm pretty sure you could not only have bought the house but also have it cleaned and at least move-in ready by the time you came home from the reception."

"All in one day?"

"Clay would have to bring in more crews, but all you'd have to do is minor renovations. They'd pull rugs, scrape away wallpaper, paint, fill some of the rooms with new furniture. The major things you could do later, but how romantic would it be to have a home to take her to after the wedding?"

I tried to imagine all of that getting done in the time we were at a wedding and couldn't. "It doesn't sound possible. I don't even own the place yet."

"You'd be shocked at how fast Clay can make things happen when he waves his magic wand. His lawyers could close on the house for you. We'd probably need a huge crew, but that's doable as well. You'd just have to keep Amanda at the wedding late." Caterina clasped her hands together in front of her in what I was beginning to recognize was an attempt to look less nervous. "I know it sounds crazy, but when the idea came to me I thought it would be beautiful because it's something we could make happen together."

"Together," I'd repeated the word.

Her eyes had shone with emotion. "You, me, and Clay. You know, as a family."

That had gutted me, but in a good way. "I'd love that. Let's make it happen." I wasn't Cooper Davis anymore, nor did I want to be. I was Cooper Landon—talking to my sister about something we could do with our brother *as a family.* We weren't on opposite sides and I didn't want Caterina to ever again feel that we were. I added, "At the wedding you'll see some strange things. Laugh along. Part of it is a prank the whole town is in on. It's not meant to embarrass anyone. We thought it might help break the ice. I'd tell you what it is, but there's a lot of effort going into it and I don't want to spoil it."

"Does Clay know?"

"No. I'll warn him if you think I should. When we planned it, I didn't realize how sensitive he is. It's not a personal prank, but it will require a certain amount of a sense of humor."

She looked across to where Clay was talking to Amanda's parents and said, "More than anything else it'll matter to him that you took his feelings into consideration. I love that you care enough to watch out for him. We never had that growing up, but I'd like to think we can be that to each other now."

With my heart thudding in my chest, I nodded. That was exactly what I wanted as well.

What happened over the last few days fell away when the song that Amanda had chosen to walk down the aisle began to play. She'd asked for the decorations to remain simple and they were. Mrs. Williams's flowers hung from the arbor beside me and the inside of the chairs that lined a silk runner Clay had supplied.

All that mattered to me was how beautiful Amanda looked when she walked into view. Her hair was styled, but loose around her shoulders. There was no poof or lace to the calf-length white dress she'd chosen. She wore simple white sandals instead of heels. It was perfectly her and I could barely breathe as she walked toward me.

The mother of the children we'd raise together.

My best friend.

My woman.

She took my hand when she joined me and we walked to

where our officiant, Everette, was standing under the arbor. Who better to marry us than someone who'd rooted for us to be together all along?

"We're gathered here today . . ." he read from the papers in his hand. As he spoke, my attention turned to the woman beaming a smile up at me. Never had I imagined love could be as pure and real as what I saw in her eyes.

"I do," I said spontaneously.

"Me too," she said without missing a beat.

Everette paused and waved his papers. "I'm not at that part yet."

I tugged Amanda forward into my arms. "I need to kiss the bride."

She laughed and wrapped her arms around my neck. "I'd be disappointed if we did this any other way."

I bent her gently back over my arm and kissed her soundly. Halfway through the kiss, we both started to laugh.

"I love you so much," she said when I lifted my head.

"You'd better," I joked, "because now you're stuck with me."

"I guess you're husband and wife now?" Everette said in confusion.

Still holding hands, Amanda and I turned back to face him. I didn't need to ask her what she wanted next, I could see it in her eyes. "No, go on, Everette."

Amanda nodded. "We don't want to miss a single part of this." She smiled at me again. "We just do things our way."

Perhaps because he'd known us both for so long, he didn't appear all that surprised when he raised his papers and began to read again.

When he asked if I had a ring for her, he looked over at her mother and winked. Dotty and Pete rose from their seats, joined us beneath the arbor, and removed their wedding rings. Dotty handed me hers. Pete gave his gold band to Amanda to hold.

In a voice meant for everyone there to hear, Dotty said, "With these rings Pete and I give our blessing to this union and the new family you've started. We could not love both of you more than we do. Take care of each other. Marriage isn't easy, but you're not in this alone."

I hugged Dotty then Pete. Amanda did the same in reverse order. When Amanda's parents returned to their seats there wasn't a dry eye in the audience.

I cleared my throat then promised to love, cherish, protect, and share my life with Amanda. She promised the same to me.

Ollie and Levi walked up with a wooden box and bags of different colored wet cement in plastic wrapping. Amanda accepted one of the bags and turned to our friends and family. "Cooper and I wanted to do something to show how our families would blend together. We considered sand, but then we wanted to make something we could all use. If everyone here could add one bag of cement to this box we're going to let it set and it will become part of the frame for a bench we'd like to put on our land. Together we've always been stronger and we've always supported each other. When you're tired, or sad, or simply need a quiet place to sit—the bench will be under a tree next to the little pond at the

Stanley place . . . hopefully soon to be our home."

She and I each poured a small bag of cement into the wooden box then kissed again. Everette said, "Now you're married."

I raised my head and laughed. "Yes."

As Amanda and I looked on, our friends and family rose to their feet to cheer then lined up to add to the box. From beside us, Everette announced, "Photos will follow the ceremony. While they're being taken, please clear away your chairs and retrieve your bullfrog from the back porch. One per family, please. You all know the rules. Unless you're keeping yours to eat, please return it after the race so it can be released back into the wild."

The crowd quieted and in true Driverton style all turned to watch my family's reaction. Caterina made a show of seeming confused by what she'd heard. Clay brought a hand to his throat and asked, "Did he just say we should retrieve a bullfrog from the back porch? Why would we want to do that?"

Everette must have heard him as well, because he said, "To participate in Driverton's traditional wedding reception bullfrog race. The winner gets to keep the flowers."

Eyes wide, Clay looked around. If I didn't know that he'd had a heads-up that something strange would happen, I would have thought he was truly shocked. "I don't touch amphibians."

His wife smiled up at him. "Today you do."

"Right." He loosened his tie. "Bullfrogs are how big?"

Mel's oldest child made a circle in the air with his hands.

"They're huge!"

"And you race them?" Caterina asked in a convincingly distressed voice.

"We do," Ollie said. "I'll help you and Benjamin choose a winner."

"That's so . . . nice of you," Benjamin said with a groan.

Amanda said, "Ollie, help them later. Clay, Lexi, Caterina, Benjamin . . . come on, let's go get the family photos done first. No one is touching me with slimy frog hands."

"Not even your husband?" I playfully reached for her.

"Not even you." She evaded my touch and laughed. "At least when it comes to frog slime."

I laughed along and was momentarily overcome by how much my perspective on life had changed in such a short time. Happiness wasn't an impossibility for me and damn, it felt good. I couldn't imagine not working with Tom to help recover children, but now I had many reasons to make sure I returned from those jobs.

Chapter Thirty-One

Amanda

BULLFROG RACING WAS hilarious.

It was hands down the funniest thing I'd ever seen my friends and family do. That they did it while attempting to look like it was something they'd done a hundred times before had me laughing so hard my sides hurt.

Cooper graciously allowed me to choose our champion. I allowed him to be the one to hold and race it. By the time we returned to the lawn where our wedding ceremony had been held, white taped lines had transformed the area into a four-laned racetrack about twenty feet long and just as wide.

Every family was allowed one "frog jockey." The rest of each family was asked to stay behind another set of lines set back from the racetrack. When we'd first discussed bullfrog racing, I hadn't imagined anyone taking it as seriously as people were. Many were googling best practices.

There were only a few rules: Be kind to the frog. Once the frog is set at the starting line, no one can touch the frog. If the frog leaves its lane, it's disqualified. The first frog to leap over the finish line is the winner of its round. There would be four rounds. At the end, four winners would race one more time for the final win.

And, no, Clay, you cannot hire someone to race for you.

Bradford and Joanna played rock, paper, scissors for which of them would race their frog. She won, then oddly gave the honor to him.

Lexi said she was a better cheerleader than jockey.

Benjamin offered to race for Caterina, but when she saw that her two siblings were racing, she took the frog from him and asked him to hold her purse.

Bradford must have done his homework, because when the race started he pounced with impressive athletic ability down onto all fours behind his frog. His hands smacked the area about six inches on either side of the frog and it jumped like an apex predator was after it.

Cooper took a similar stance, but less aggressive. His frog jumped, but not nearly as far as Bradford's had.

Caterina was in a dress which definitely inhibited her movements. She remained standing and encouraged her frog to jump by clapping and leaping behind it. It quickly did a side jump into Clay's lane.

Clay delayed the start of his race by wasting precious seconds inspecting whatever residue the frog had left on his hands and wiping it off with an antibacterial wipe before making similar moves to what Caterina had done. When his frog didn't move he dropped to his hands and knees and clapped directly behind it.

Mel, our official photographer that day, captured the joy on Clay's face when his bullfrog leapt an impressive third of the track. When I saw the photo, I knew it would forever hang on a wall in our home because it was in that moment that Clay became one of us. He wasn't at all fazed when we told him this was the first time any of us had raced frogs and that it had been a little prank. Everyone was impressed with how amused he was by the whole thing.

Bradford won the first round and the championship. No one was surprised. As nice as he'd been to us, there was something about him that even a bullfrog understood shouldn't be messed with.

Everette's family collected the frogs after the race, awarded the title of Top Bullfrog Jockey of the Year to Bradford and we all washed our hands with soap and water from a hose. In that time, the area transformed again to one with round tables, a dance floor, and Mike's DJ sound system.

Cooper and I danced the first song alone, then were joined by other couples for the next few. The reception was somewhat traditional, but we did serve the cake before the meal . . . just because . . . and it was perfect that way too.

Clay was disappointed by the news that Mary, Levi's love interest, had chosen to not attend the wedding. Mrs. Williams offered to pair up with Clay to look into that situation.

We stayed late at the wedding and that was fine with me. I liked that Cooper wanted to stay to ensure my parents weren't left with a mess. I did wonder why he seemed to be stalling at the very end, but that concern fell away when Cooper asked me if I was ready for my wedding present.

I immediately said yes, but part of me felt sad that I hadn't gotten him something until he explained the gift was really from his family and him. Side by side in the old truck my father had given Cooper, we left my parents' house. With his hand in mine, I asked Cooper, "Are you going to tell me where we're going?"

"Do you want me to?"

I bit my bottom lip. "Yes and no. I'm dying of curiosity, but I already have everything I ever wanted so I know that whatever it is, as long as I share it with you, I'll love it."

Cooper raised my hand to his lips and kissed it. "That's how I feel about everything that's going on. Our lives are about to change. Some of it more than I'm sure we can even imagine, but this is what's important to me." He looked me in the eye, then quickly glanced down at my stomach before returning his attention to the road. "Us."

"Yes." There were so many unknowns, but our love for each other wasn't one of them. "You've always made me feel safe and I hope I do the same for you."

His hand tightened on mine. "Speaking of safety, when I talk to Bradford and Ian about what it would mean to join their 'team,' I want you there. Caterina believes they take on jobs that others can't and there's some risk involved in that. Before I say yes, I'll need to know you're okay with it."

I'd have to be, because when you love a hero you don't ask him to be less, you celebrate that he is more. "Thank you for that, Cooper. I'm sure I will be." I took a deep breath and added, "Is it crazy to wish you weren't rich? At least not the kind of rich I think you are."

He glanced my way again. "First of all, what's mine is yours, so we're both wealthy now. Second, talk to me. What part of this scares you?"

It was a good question. "When I think of people with that kind of money, I imagine secret meetings where they decide the future of humanity. I know it's probably all conspiracy theories, but I don't want to be in that role."

He sighed, which I took as him acknowledging he wasn't sure he wanted to be either. "I felt powerless when I couldn't help Shawn's mother more. We could do some real good with these resources."

"That kind of power can go to a person's head. Do we really want it?"

"Alone, I'd be worried, but I have you, and we have your family, and together we have Driverton. They'll keep us grounded." He let out a slow breath. "I've seen evil. I've fought it. I've won and I've lost to it. Money doesn't make people evil, and it doesn't make evil people good. It's just a tool. I have no idea if rich people actually have secret meetings where they plot the demise or salvation of humanity, but if they do, we want a seat at that table. If there is some master plot against humanity, we'll uncover it, and stop it."

I put a hand on my stomach. "That's a little terrifying, but I agree. Regular people like you and I need to know."

He placed my other hand on his thigh and laid his over it. "I'm not looking to go to war. I intend to stick around to raise our kids and grow old with you. Whatever we do, we'll do carefully and not alone."

I loved that given power, my man wasn't looking to plunder. He wasn't and never had been a pirate. He was a dolphin, choosing to use his opportunities to save people rather than win the game.

Or maybe that's how the game is won . . . by choosing the kinder path.

It was dark when we pulled up to the Stanley place. I first thought that his surprise would be something he gave me inside our mobile home. Only when we parked in front of the house did I notice that it looked freshly painted.

"Did you buy the Stanley house?" I asked, sitting forward in my seat to see better.

"It's officially the Landon house now."

"How?" I whipped around and asked in a rush.

"With a little help from my family. Okay, a lot of help."

"Oh, my God, you're amazing." I warmed from head to toe and fell in love with Cooper all over again. "You had it painted too."

Cooper parked. "Clay made that possible. There's still a lot that'll need to be done to the home, but if the workers did what they said they would, we should be able to comfortably stay here tonight."

He stepped out and walked around to let me out, but I met him halfway and jumped into his arms. What the inside did or didn't look like didn't matter as much as the thought and love that had gone into his gift. "I love you, Cooper Landon."

He ran his hands through my hair and between kisses said, "I love you too, Amanda Landon."

"Thank you for giving me a home."

"Thank you for giving me a family to come home to."

Hand in hand we walked into our new home and tears

began pouring down my cheeks. He pulled me to his side. "Hey, hey, no crying."

I sniffed and wiped at my face. "Pregnant women are allowed to be emotional," I joked.

He turned me, kissed my forehead, and murmured, "And their husbands?"

I beamed a smile up at him. "They handle it all with stoic strength. Happily planning how they'll share the night feeding schedule."

He chuckled. "That must be why I also had the room next to ours made into the baby's room."

"You didn't." My heart thudded wildly as a wave of wonder washed over me. He'd thought of everything.

"I did. Well, one of the crews Clay flew in did." He ducked his head in humble acceptance of my praise. "I had it cleaned out and refreshed but not decorated. Mel said mothers choose themes for things like that—"

I cut him off with a hungry kiss then paused. "Cooper Landon, how is it possible for me to fall more in love with you every single day?"

"I've been asking myself the same thing since the first time we met." He flipped on a light at the top of the stairs. It lit, blinked, then went out. After a pause he said, "Well, we can either explore the upstairs in the dark or fuck down here then return to the camper tonight and check out the renovations tomorrow."

I wiggled my eyebrows at him. "Those stairs look freshly carpeted."

We shared a laugh then a heated look. Life with Cooper

was full of the unexpected. It was scary, messy, exciting, and so damn wonderful . . . exactly the way life was supposed to be.

The End

Printed in Great Britain
by Amazon